PENGUIN BOOKS

Supporting Cast

Praise for *My Name is Leon*

'My debut of the year so far . . . heartbreaking and warm
at the same time' *Stylist*

'Tender and heartbreaking' Rachel Joyce, bestselling
author of *The Unlikely Pilgrimage of Harold Fry*

'Vivid and endearing – a very powerful book'
Emma Healey, author of *Elizabeth is Missing*

'Authentic and beautiful, urgent and honest, this novel does
what only the best do: it quietly makes room in your heart'
Chris Cleave, author of *Everyone Brave is Forgiven*

'Beautiful and heartbreaking – I cried buckets of tears
for Leon and his family' Cathy Rentzenbrink,
author of *The Last Act of Love*

'The unforgettable story of a boy struggling to belong.
Heartbreaking and uplifting – just read it' *Daily Mail*

Praise for *A Trick to Time*

'A love story to take on the classics' *Emerald Street*

'An emotionally sure-handed novel exploring harrowing
terrain with . . . sensitivity' *Sunday Times*

'Excellent. The novel's ending will leave you reeling'
Daily Mail

'An unforgettable tale of grief and life-long love'
Woman's Own

'Tender with a fierce undercurrent of tension and heartbreak'
Jane Shemilt, author of *Daughter*

'Moving and enlightening' *Independent*

'*The Trick to Time* proves that Kit de Waal is a writer destined
for even greater things' *Red*

Supporting Cast

KIT DE WAAL

PENGUIN BOOKS

PENGUIN BOOKS

UK | USA | Canada | Ireland | Australia
India | New Zealand | South Africa

Penguin Books is part of the Penguin Random House group of companies
whose addresses can be found at global.penguinrandomhouse.com.

First published 2020
001

Copyright © Kit de Waal, 2020

The moral right of the author has been asserted

Set in 12.5/14.75 pt Garamond MT Std
Typeset by Jouve (UK), Milton Keynes
Printed and bound in Great Britain by Clays Ltd, Elcograf S.p.A.

A CIP catalogue record for this book is available from the British Library

ISBN: 978-0-241-97342-4

For Marnie, Vincent, Kaodi, Ella, Reuben,
Harper and Vaughan with love

✳ CASTLIST ✳

CAROL RYCROFT
Bristol, 1981

CRAZY ROSE
91 Morecambe Crescent, October 2018

SYLVIA
Leighton Buzzard bypass, 1965

WOBBLY BOBBY
Moseley Village, 2019

BYRON FRANCIS
Lincoln Prison, 4 September 1983

MR DEVLIN
Dublin, 1952

JUDY SUTHERLAND 'THE ZEBRA'
Shipstone Close, 1990

CASTRO
Springfield Police Station, 1981

BECKY FINCH
Staff canteen, Morrisons, 2016

NICOLA WRIGHT
At home, Cambridge, 2011

EDITH PAISLEY -JONES
(WOMAN IN A FLOWERY SKIRT)
Allotments, 1981

MARGARET MACNAUGHTON 'PESTILENCE'
Clarinbridge, Galway, 1953

TRISH
Hastings, Christmas 2018

ADAM ALBRIGHT
West Bay, August 2001

ELISABETH GRÄFIN VON EVERSTEIN -OHSEN
(MOTHER OF ANDREAS)
Wellingsbüttel, Hamburg, 2016

KARL
Rue Lepic, Paris, autumn 1990

DR ROBERT WRIGHT
Golden Vale retirement home, 2018

GAYLE
Eastbourne District General Hospital, 2 February 1981

CORNELIA MACNAUGHTON
Kilcolgan, Galway, 1979

BRIDIE O'CONNOR
Kilmore Quay, Wexford, 1952

WILLIAM MACNAUGHTON
Clarinbridge, Galway, 1972

BIG TOM FALLON
St Bridget's Hall, Skibbereen, Cork, 1983

Carol Rycroft

Bristol, 1981

A blinking neon sign promised BED & BREAKFAST, BUDGET ROOMS. On. Off. On. Off. Carol climbed the steps between the crumbling plaster columns and walked in. The hotel smelt of cigarettes and damp, and as soon as she stepped on the mat inside the front door, a bell rang and a head appeared through a hatch in the lobby. The head was round and hairless and chamois-leather beige. It wore a smile.

'Help you, love?' The man leant on his elbows as though he expected a long conversation, but Carol wanted only a single room for a single night.

'First floor,' he said. 'Number three, seven quid. Or,' he said, dropping his voice to a whisper, 'top floor, private bathroom, no sharing nothing, and I can let you have that for a tenner today cos we're quiet.'

He twisted his neck so he could see the little tartan case she had in her hands. 'Visiting someone?'

Carol nodded and slid her purse out of her pocket. She found a note and told him the first floor would be fine and could she possibly borrow the Yellow Pages?

He gave her a key and poked the fat yellow book through the hatch. 'It's a bit out of date, sweetheart. Need anything in particular?'

'Just looking,' she answered as if she was browsing through a rail of blouses. Her voice in her own ears sounded small and unconvincing, so she tried a smile. 'I just want to see what's on,' she added.

'Oh, you should have said,' said the beige man, and he unlatched a door and shuffled out. He was smaller than Carol and she realized he must have been standing on something behind the hatch, something he kept for feeling tall and greeting customers. He pointed at a display rack on the wall behind her and began to rifle through some leaflets.

'This is Bristol, darlin', it ain't London. We've got gardens, museums and art galleries. We ain't got palaces and we ain't got shows.'

Carol took the shiny bits of paper but kept hold of the Yellow Pages and thanked him for his help.

'You need anything, love, you just trot back here to Maurice. I'm your man. Maurice.'

The room was small and dark with wallpaper that had once been bright and busy. A blue nylon eiderdown hung unevenly on a single bed and a washbasin in the corner of the room caught the noisy drip from an old tap. Carol went straight to the window, but it had been painted shut. She had no idea where she was, she couldn't see a single street sign, but she was in Bristol at least and that made her two hours and a hundred miles nearer Tony.

She looked up the road as far as she could see. There were cars and vans and lorries creeping past and buses lined up like giant toys. It wasn't like her high street, the shops here with their insides spilt out on the pavement, boxes full of strange vegetables, dirty greens, dull reds. The noises and smells of the street coiled together and slithered through a long crack that ran across the window like a scar. Everything was loud, everyone was moving to the rhythm of the bass belting out of the crawling cars and eating things as they walked along. Below her window a Chinese man was dishing out cartons of fried food that smelt sickly sweet.

Carol remembered Tina's stinging words before she left.

'He's left you, Carol. You have to accept it.'

Suddenly she noticed a little boy holding on to his mother's coat. He was too near the kerb. Carol wanted to bang her fists on the glass or dash downstairs, sweep him up in her arms and save him, never let him go. She realized then that she had her forehead pressed against the window and it had begun to mist up and everything was becoming blurred and fuzzy. She felt a stab of panic.

Still in her coat, Carol sat on the bed and put the Yellow Pages on her lap. She found the pen and paper she had packed in her bag and turned to Snooker Halls. That's what Tony's friend had said, that Tony had a new job in a snooker hall. There were four pages of snooker halls and just looking at them made her feel better. In one of those snooker halls she would find Tony. What a surprise he'd get.

Some of the adverts had pictures and said they were open twenty-four hours. She turned the page and found a long list of Private Snooker Halls, some of them offering free membership. Carol wondered how much they were paying Tony and if he had managed to save anything because when they moved in together they might need a deposit. She remembered she'd had to break into a five-pound note at the station cafe and ask three times for a cup of tea and really she could have done without the cup of tea, she just needed to sit down. There would be none of that when she and Tony were saving up.

Carol turned another page. Some of the snooker halls said there was a restaurant on site and some of them held monthly competitions, some of them said 'Private', some of them added 'Poker Tables' and some of them had 'Billiards and Pool'. While she was on the train Carol had made a plan, but she felt like she was forgetting a really big part of it. She undid the buttons on her coat and turned another page. The print was smaller, difficult to read, and the rows were dense with bold, black ink. Some of the adverts had slogans and said 'Free Lounge', and all of them promised a 'Warm Welcome'. Carol looked around to see if there was a radiator on in the room, to find out where the heat was coming from – something was sucking her dry. She'd done nothing more than sit on the train for two hours, but she felt like she'd done the whole journey on foot over hills and mountains.

She flicked through the remaining pages, trying to concentrate. One snooker hall said she could bring a guest and another told her that ladies played for free. Carol read every advert and then she closed the thick yellow book.

It was very strange what happened then. It was like a very bad person put their hand on Carol's shoulder and whispered something so horrible and frightening that she wanted to die. Carol stood up. She knew she had to stand up and she had to run away from the terrible feeling that had come into the room. But she couldn't move. She dropped the Yellow Pages and she put her hands in her pockets and started picking at the lining.

Then Carol sat down again. She sat down and she stayed sitting down until the lights came on in the street, she stayed sitting down until the lights went off and the morning came, and then she got up and went to the toilet down the hall. Walking down the hall was the hardest thing Carol had ever done, but she didn't want to wet the bed.

When she got back to her room, she locked the door and started to cry. Carol didn't make any noise but inside she was screaming and screaming and screaming. The air was full of ugly, spiteful vapour and the hand on her shoulder was pressing down. Then the beige man knocked the door.

'All right, love? Checkout's at ten but if you want the room for another night you can have it cos no one else is booked in.'

Carol picked up her suitcase, opened the door and walked past him down the stairs. He shouted after her, but Carol had no idea what he said. On the street she was in everyone's way, people were looking at her like she was different from them, like they knew she had a bad hand on her shoulder. When she started to cry again, an old woman stopped her.

'Are you all right, love?'

Carol kept walking. She saw two women in a launderette. One was folding a shirt and the other was smiling, so Carol opened the door and sat on the wooden bench by the washing machines. But the feeling had followed her into the launderette with its soft white sheets and fresh blue soap powder where nothing bad had ever happened to anyone. It was hovering over her like the shadow of the devil and Carol held tightly on to the bench because even though she was sitting down she thought she was going to fall over. She gripped and swayed and then she felt the room explode and she let go.

'My name's Carol,' she said.

A man wearing jeans and a lumberjack shirt told her he was a nurse, but Carol didn't believe him.

'Okay, Carol. Do you know why you're here?'

'No.'

Do you know how you got here?'

'No.'

'Do you know how long you've been here?'

'No.'

'Okay, Carol. We'll get to that in a moment.' He smiled and knitted his fingers together. 'Tell me what you remember?'

Carol realized then that she was in someone else's clothes and her hair was parted on the wrong side. She was sitting in a chair near a barred window in a small room with a poster of a waterfall on the wall and the door closed.

'I was just sitting down and they had the heating right up. It was really hot and then I fainted.'

'Well, actually, Carol, you collapsed.'

'Did I?'

'Yes, you did. Can you remember anything else?'

Carol felt like she had a secret inside her, but she had no idea what it was. 'I think something bad happened.'

'Something happened to you? Can you remember what it was?'

'No.'

'Okay, Carol. Well, I can fill in some of the blanks for you and that might help you remember. First of all, you collapsed five days ago and when you woke up you were very distressed. You haven't been well for the past five days and we've had to sedate you. Today's the first day that you've been able to talk to us.'

'Five days?'

'Yes, five days. How do you feel today, Carol? Are you feeling better?'

'I feel like something bad's going to happen.'

Carol stood up and then she sat down again. She wanted to tear off the clothes that didn't belong to her and put her parting right. No, she didn't want to put the parting right, she wanted to pull the hair right off. Maybe it didn't belong to her either.

'I'm beginning to get frightened now. You're scaring me because you keep asking me to talk about it.' Carol knew she was shouting, but she wanted him to stop asking her about the bad hand and the bad secret. The nurse stood up and handed her a small cup of water and two pale-pink tablets.

'That's it,' he said as she swallowed them.

The nurse said she was going to feel better soon, but it was eight more days before Carol could remember enough information for them to contact Social Services, who contacted Tina from the upstairs maisonette, and another twenty-four hours before Tina could make the trip to come and get her.

'You haven't got a scrap of fat on you, Carol.'

Tina looked worried like she was trying not to cry.

They sat together in the over-bright hospital canteen. Carol had her check suitcase and Tina clutched her handbag with the gold clasp that she only used for a night out on her birthday. Tina kept mentioning Carol's weight and her hair. There were tears on Tina's cheek and dry tracks the previous ones had made in her thick, ivory foundation.

'You could do with a proper dinner, Carol, and this tea's not up to much, is it? Want something else? A soft drink?'

'No. I want to go home.'

Carol's flat was all boarded up because someone had gone inside and taken all her stuff. Tina warned Carol before they got there and said she was sorry for not keeping a better eye on it and said she could stay in Bobby's room for a few nights. But the same day, Social Services came and said she had a room at the Maybird Centre and they gave her a key.

The Maybird Centre was near the dual carriageway and the cars went past on a flyover. Carol looked out of the window and could see right inside the cars, see people going to their jobs, see people arguing. Carol kept waiting for everything to go back to normal, but before she put the light out that night she took two of her tablets and sat on the edge of the bed waiting for them to work, waiting for the thick wooziness of oblivion that would eventually settle her nerves, like a heavy blanket on barbed wire.

In the morning, she went back to Tina's house.

'I've put a sugar in your coffee, Carol. You need something inside you if you won't eat.'

'I'm not hungry.'

'Carol, you're not going to get any better if you don't eat.' After a pause, Tina sat down, clutching a tea towel.

'It was a crazy idea, Carol. Chasing a good-for-nothing bloke halfway round the country. No wonder you've had a breakdown. It's not just the baby blues this time, Carol.'

'Baby blues?'

'Jake, Carol. Jake.'

And then Carol knew what the bad secret was and why she had been hunted and found and tortured and punished. She began to cry, so they held one another for a few minutes.

'Oh, Carol, don't cry. It'll be all right.'

Tina refilled the kettle and took a loaf of bread out of the cupboard. 'Here's what we do. We go to Social Services tomorrow morning and find out where they are, Jake and Leon, and we'll get them back. That's it. That's our plan.'

Tina made a hasty wipe of her face with the tea towel and refolded it in half. 'Come on, Carol, drink your tea. Have a bit of toast. Don't cry. It's going to be all right.'

But Carol wasn't all right for seventeen weeks. On the last day of the eighteenth week, Social Services told her that her children were in care because she had abandoned them. It was obvious they knew she had the bad hand on her shoulder, so she left and went back home to the Maybird Centre.

On the twenty-third week she went back to Social Services and they told her she needed an assessment to see if she could look after her children again. If she felt able, they said, she could visit them at the Family Centre with a social worker to supervise, but Carol went back home to her room and got her new benefit book and she worked out that in two weeks' time she would have enough to go back to Bristol.

She would get the right Yellow Pages this time and get every address of every snooker hall and work her way through them, a different one every night. He would be there and she would find him.

Crazy Rose

91 Morecambe Crescent, October 2018

He brings blossom in April, perfume in the summer, scents of sizzling meat from nearby gardens, and sometimes he carries music that makes her close her eyes and press her heart. He brings her little presents, scraps of things that he eddies from the street into her porch – a chocolate wrapper, a pigeon feather, faded print. Without him, no one would call.

It's late morning when she opens the front door to see what he has brought her. He blusters in.

'What have we today?' she asks, gathers up his offerings and sits by the fire. There is always something to make her smile. A polystyrene carton smells of sour fish. He has tumbled it all the way from town, from a young man who drank late with his friends, who laughed with his mouth full, who kissed a girl with vinegar fingers and loved her that night.

There is also a letter, ten words of it, unfinished, written in ink, screwed up small, footprints on the back.

Dear Faith, it reads, *I'm writing to say sorry, if you would just . . .*

She goes to the door again to see if he has brought her the rest, but there is nothing, and that night, before she goes to bed, she hears him, rattling the letter box, strong fingers at the sash windows. She only has half the story, so she'll have to be patient. She folds the letter in half and tucks it between the magazines and books in the paper mountain behind her chair.

But this summer he hardly visits and her house is quiet. Her dinners are delivered and a young man comes and holds her hand. They want to look after her, he says, and make room for her in Holly Lodge. But he doesn't tell her what Holly Lodge is and he doesn't come back. She is alone again.

Then one day the wind is back with his October gift, hidden under the free newspaper. Two golden leaves holding hands at the stem, the colour of warm sand, tipped with blood red, spots of green that have refused to fade. She holds them up to the light, traces their thin veins, useless now, carrying nothing. She'll dry them out by the gas fire until they turn crisp and brittle and crumble in her hand.

She begins to worry about winter when he cries a lot, gets angry, blows the slates off the roof, howls too long and keeps her awake. But at least he's a bit of company and she turns to look around the room at his many little gifts and she remembers the half-letter that came in spring.

Dear Faith

She's careful when she stands, careful when she tugs bits of paper from the mountain, careful when she steadies its lean. It starts with a little shudder and the slide of old magazines from the top that land on her shoulder and end at her feet. Then a dozen cereal boxes, ones she flattened and folded and carefully stowed. Then a car magazine and a poster for a missing cat and a flyer for Labour, then the slippery slide of pages and pages of colourful coupons and offers from the new supermarket she's never seen, a walk and a bus journey away. And then a tumble, then an avalanche, and the mountain groans and shifts and bullies her backwards until she's standing on the leaves and singeing the back of her skirt.

The gas fire whispers and tells her to be careful. And just as she's about to turn it off, in he comes. A whisper at first, then a rattle of the glass and then a whoosh and a quick dance around the mountain and he's alive. Yellow and white now. Blue when he catches the paper. Red where he curls the plastic. Hot and wild, filling the room with his crackles and hisses and his thick, grey breath.

She opens wide. He fills her throat. Devours her.

Sylvia

Leighton Buzzard bypass, 1965

It's forty-seven minutes from Leighton Buzzard to Luton on the number 136. I've got myself a neat perch, top deck, front, new estate off to the left, biscuit factory to the right. It'll be all green soon, fields and trees for miles and miles, and at the rate this bus is rattling along I'm going to be late on top of everything else. And it stinks: old leather, old tobacco, old sweat, old perfume, old people.

The bus conductor gave me the once-over when I got on. I know what he's thinking: 'Pretty girl but she's had her thirtieth birthday about five times in a row.' He's seen a good silk headscarf from Bassetts, a wool coat with a penny collar, lovely pair of patent kitten heels and a clasp-top handbag and he's thinking, 'Vogue Road.' When he comes to collect my fare, he'll look down at me and he'll see the lines around my eyes, the puffiness you always get if you've been crying in the night, and he'll think, 'No, Hangover Square.' He'd be right.

Should have bought fags at the newsagent. I've only got eight. Not enough for this journey and then an hour with that solicitor. A woman solicitor they said on the phone. You wouldn't credit it, would you? Never expected that. Not in Bedfordshire at any rate. Maybe you get more sympathy with a woman. Maybe that's why she went into divorce law. Maybe when she was at university she had half an eye on her boyfriend, imagined him doing the dirty on her one day, and she thought to herself, 'I'll make sure I know what's what when the time comes.' Because the time always comes.

Going to dye my hair on Saturday. I can do it myself for half the price of Diane's. Fair enough, it takes a bit longer and you have to make sure you get someone to help you with the back, but our Mo will do that. She'll be quick about it as well because she can't stand the smell of dye when she's expecting. Dye, bleach, window cleaner, vinegar, lemons, nutmeg and tomato soup. What they've got in common, God knows, but it was the same last time except she added shoe polish and lavender to the mix.

'Oh, it's never cake and biscuits, is it, Sylv?' she says and puts both hands on her backside. Then Roy comes in and slips his hands round any bit of waist he can find and kisses her because Roy don't see and Roy don't care.

I thought it would rain today. Rain and hail and lightning. Never expected a sunny day and blossom on the trees.

I've got my marriage certificate and birth certificate, mine and his. I've got a note of the date he left and I've brought cash if she wants paying up front. Mo told me to just stick to the facts.

'I'm your sister, Sylv,' she said. 'You moan to me and you cry to me and we can go over it as many times as you like because that's my job. But you're paying by the hour so stick to the facts.'

Easy for her to say with Roy as dotty about her now as he was ten years ago, worse maybe.

I was seventeen and our Mo was eighteen. There we were in the Majestic Ballroom, nearly Christmas. Big band. It was me Roy asked to dance first. Me. Brian was stood behind him, tapping his foot to the music with his hands in his pockets. So I had a dance with Roy and then he asked our Mo, so Brian had no choice but to ask me. Course, as soon as we were on the dance floor it was a done deal. I mean, the pair of us looked like bloody film stars and he didn't make a move I couldn't follow.

In five minutes there was only the two of us out there. It's like we'd been rehearsing somewhere, rehearsing for this moment. 'Sylvia and Brian, Stars of Tomorrow.' People talked about us for months. I used to imagine articles in the paper about how we met that night and how we danced in the middle of a clapping circle and how the sweat made my dress cling, how our hands were so slippery we could hardly hold on, but he spun me round and caught me again like he'd never let me go. I trusted him, fell right back towards the floor knowing he'd be there. I wrote all these articles in my head because I thought, I really, really thought, that one day someone would ask me about it because we'd be famous and a journalist would take his pad out and say, 'How did you two meet?' and I'd have something already prepared.

I was right, sort of. We did have a man from the *Leighton Examiner* asking questions because in the end it was a double wedding, two sisters marrying two brothers, but it was Roy did all the talking and obviously it was about him and Mo. Brian was drunk.

Maureen looked about as beautiful as anybody I've ever seen. We chose the same pattern and had it made up, a copy of a Christian Dior like Princess Margaret wore on her tour of the West Indies, the one with the pleated skirt, off-the-shoulder bodice. Neither of us wanted to splash out on the full white dress affair because that's a frock you only wear once and we both had homes to set up. The only thing we did different was the headpiece. Mo had a tiny pink cloche with a white satin band and I had a netted pillbox in pale blue. We had a photograph album each in raw silk that came in a white box with gold edging. Mr and Mrs Brian Hargreaves. Fourteen shillings.

I'm going to start wearing that bloody dress again. Trim the sleeves and the hem with gingham and add a belt. Might take some of the volume out of that skirt as well, make it a bit more fashionable. Wear it with a shrug or a cardigan on a bright day. Day like today. Sort of day you should be somewhere nice.

I do love the seaside. We used to take our holidays together every year, the four of us, Roy and Mo, me and Brian. We'd have the whole factory fortnight, caravan or lodgings, Skegness or Hastings. Woolacombe one year, which was lovely. Then our mum died and Mo said she felt like an orphan and wanted kids. I didn't feel ready and I told Brian I wanted to wait. He didn't mind one way or the other, but we had a row about it all the same. He went to the pub and didn't come back that night.

First time it happens, you think the worst. He's dead. Robbed. Stabbed. Lying under the wheel of a car. Heart attack. Arrested. Then he slinks in at six in the morning and I hear him creeping upstairs because I haven't slept a bloody wink, have I?

I've stopped crying by now and I'm good and ready with a right mouthful. I'm watching the bedroom door, fag in hand, when slowly, inch by inch, a baby doll appears. He's only gone and nicked it from someone's bloody dustbin, from God-knows-where, a bloody baby doll with half its hair burnt off and one blinking eye. No Brian anywhere to be seen, just a naked doll, wobbling from side to side, making this daft crying.

'Waaaw! Waaaw! Don't hit me, Mummy! I'm ever so sorry! Waaaw!'

I had to stop myself laughing and when I don't say anything he carries on, 'Love you, Mummy. Waaaw!'

Soft beggar. I must have let out a little snigger because all of a sudden he chucks the doll into the air and jumps into bed, stinking of The Poacher's Arms, and that's that. He's got away with it.

Mo fell pregnant straight away. Out he pops one Saturday morning, David Royston Hargreaves, taking us all by surprise, eight and a half pounds. When I saw the size of that bloody kid, it put me off, to be honest. I imagined it all scrunched up inside me, folded in half and sucking its thumb, and I thought, no, I can't do it. I just don't think I'm the mothering kind. I poured all that sort of stuff into my husband.

Anyway, here comes our David, one week to the day before the anniversary of our mum's death. Mo said it softened the blow. Lovely boy, he was. Is. Seven now. Grammar school material if you ask me. I'm a godmother. That poor boy's got me. I told Mo not to be soft. I said, ask our Barbara, she's the oldest cousin. Or Valerie, who's practically a bloody nun, but Mo's her own person, she just carried on, booked the christening, booked the church hall, and that was that. Brian said he was delighted to be godfather. Delighted, he said. Delighted. I can still see him smirking behind that newspaper. 'I'll show him a thing or two when the time comes.'

The thing is, when I was talking to Mo about Brian the other day, she said something that really made me think. She said that no matter how things were right now it was important that I remember the good times. If I just concentrate on all his bad points then it's like I've wasted ten years of my life, it's like it was all a mistake, like every day was full of unhappiness, and it wasn't.

'You loved him, Sylv,' she said. 'And he loved you. And even if it's not like that now, you have to remember the sunshine.'

So, it's August Bank Holiday and it's bloody baking. You'd have thought we'd pitched up in Spain or somewhere foreign, not West Beach in Littlehampton. It's so hot there's people fainting and the roads are melting and dogs are dying in cars. We've got a room in a lovely little boarding house right on the front with the sun bouncing off every wall.

Two years married, we are, and we're still head over heels, still hand in hand, me on his lap or the two of us lying in the quiet after we've made love. Sometimes, we take little trips to quiet country inns where nobody knows us. We don't need the radio or the jukebox or anything. Brian says I'm all the music he needs.

'You're like rock 'n' roll and a lullaby all rolled into one,' he says. 'Look at you.' He holds his fists up, ducks right and left, and then cuffs me under the chin. 'Bam bam!' he says. 'You're a bloody knock-out, you are, Sylvie.'

We get to Littlehampton late on Friday night, so that first morning we just stay in bed, smoking and kissing and laughing and talking, listening to the street come alive, watching the nets dance in the breeze. The landlady comes up twice and raps on the door.

'Room twelve?' she says. 'You've missed breakfast.'

Brian groans and swoons back on the pillow like he's dying of starvation and she hears me giggle. 'Well!' she says and stamps along the lino and all the way down the stairs. She must have told all the other boarders because the next morning everyone's staring and tutting. One woman shakes her head and purses her lips.

'How do, love!' shouts Brian, slaps his hands together and plonks himself at the biggest table in the middle of the room. Then halfway through his bacon and eggs, he points his knife at me and says, 'What did you say your name was?' He's a right bugger.

We get ourselves a lovely spot down on the beach, leaning against the sea wall. I've brought the blue towels out of our room and some of that new Ambre Solaire Extreme Tanning Oil with Coconut. I'm determined to go back home brown as a berry. Brian's always tanned – ridiculous, he is. Summer or winter, he looks like a film star on a cruise ship.

'Mother had a thing for our Indian doctor,' he says with a wink. 'I reckon he slipped her some special medicine.'

I've bought us a fresh loaf, a bit of salad and cooked ham, and I've tucked it under some pebbles so we don't die of food poisoning. We've got lemonade and a couple of bottles of brown ale.

'We'll stick to shandy for now. Let's not peak too soon, duck,' says Brian, portioning it out, but I notice mine was a good bit weaker than his.

Then all of a sudden we both turn and look out to sea. I don't know what it is. Something in the air, a terrible cold feeling or like when dogs hear them high-pitched sounds that humans can't. We both stand up. There's lots of people doing the same, looking far out at the horizon with their hands shielding the sun. I start walking slowly to the water's edge and so does Brian, but then he's running past me. He's running into the water and ripping off his shirt.

People are pointing now and one lady on the beach is hopping up and down, saying, 'Help him! Help him!' She's pointing and screaming and I can see now, far, far out, a boy about nine or ten flailing about and waving. But my Brian is already swimming, chopping through the water like a propeller, his arms going over and over, cutting and slicing and kicking his legs, and he's almost there, almost, almost, and then he disappears. Both of them are gone. I stare at the last spot I saw him, but he doesn't come back up. Nothing. The boy is drowned and my Brian is dead.

It was one moment. Half a moment. A quarter. But then again, it's for ever and it's always. It's long enough to know that I will never be the same, never know happiness again, never not love him, that I will miss him all the days of my life.

I must have sunk down on to my knees in the sand because someone kneels next to me and says, 'Look! He's got him!' And further along the beach Brian is dragging the boy out of the sea. I can't move and I can't see anything because they've crowded around him, but afterwards I heard about what Brian did, how he pressed the water out of the boy's lungs and made his heart beat and gave him the kiss of life. How he turned him on his side and let the sea drain out of the corner of his mouth. How he handed that boy back to his mother, alive and crying.

Brian's soaking wet. His trousers are ruined and his hair is plastered down but he just picks up his shirt and takes me by the hand back to where we've got our things.

He flops back on to the blue towel and says, 'Pour us a drink, love.'

I keep looking at him, I keep looking at his trousers and wondering if they're dry clean only. I keep looking at him, alive and breathing, and wondering if our Mo will know how to dry a leather belt, and I want to start praying or something. I can hardly keep myself straight, but Brian doesn't like a fuss, so I do as I'm told and take the lid off a bottle of beer.

He glugs it back in about three seconds and then he falls asleep or pretends to. People keep coming up all the time, wanting to shake his hand, but I put a finger on my lips and wave them away. We have drinks bought us all that night in the pub by the posh hotel and someone stands up and makes a little speech.

'We've got a hero amongst us,' he says and nods at Brian, who raises his glass. I can feel his hand tighter and tighter on mine, hating every minute of it.

We never talked about what he did and I knew without him ever saying that I was not to mention it when we got back home. I couldn't ever tell him how proud I was.

I couldn't tell him about that terrible moment when I couldn't see him in the water. I couldn't tell him that there's a mother somewhere just like our Mo, who would have had her heart broken if it wasn't for what he did.

So I just said what I always said. 'You'll be the death of me, Brian Hargreaves.'

Wobbly Bobby

Moseley Village, 2019

Fuck me, Bobby, mate, you've dropped a few stone. Nearly didn't recognize you. Long time no see. You still up Talbot Street?

Really? Bloody hell, Bob, Dickens Heath? That new estate with the bungalows? Yeah, I was working on them. Must have cost a bit to move up there. Your missus is from that way, isn't she?

Me? Linda? Nah, nah, Bob, mate. She fucked off, didn't she? Took the kids and pissed off to Liverpool with some new bloke. Stopped me seeing them. My youngest will have forgotten me by now. Keep thinking I'm going to go up there and surprise them. Not that I've got her address or anything. I had to move back with my mum when she left. Had to sell the house and give her seventy-five per cent. Can you credit it? Seventy-five bloody per cent. It's a fucking killer. Lost everything. But you can't feel sorry for yourself, can you? Just got to get on with it. What about you, Bobby? How's the kids?

Jesus, university? Both of them? Can't believe it. Makes you feel ancient. We're getting old, Bobby. We'll be creaking about the place soon.

Know what you mean, Bob. I can hardly move when I get home these days. Eight hours on the shovel. And my wrists starting to go. A building site's no place for a man over forty. But I just put a day's graft in then text Mitch and Stovie when I get home. Remember Stovie? Divorced now but po-faced as ever. Everyone used to think it was his bird that put that face on him but he's just a miserable git with or without her. That's the thing about you, Bobby, mate. You're always happy. Don't know how you do it. Sorry to hear about your dad, by the way. He was a good bloke when he wasn't chasing you with a length of curtain wire. How's your mum?

Say that again, didn't catch it?

Spain? Spain as in Spain? You're kidding. Permanent, like? Auntie Tina in Spain? She'll love that.

So, that's you with your holidays sorted then. Lucky bastard. Still see any of the others? Jimmy or Creep or Fat Nolan or that lot?

Creep got married? Who'd have him? Is she mail order or something? Nah, I didn't get invited, mate. Don't really see much of them, to be honest. You're like the hub, Bob. Middle of the wheel. The good guy. How's the legs?

Did you get a ramp fitted then?

It's a nice chair anyway, Bob. Must have cost a bit. Remember that one you had when we were kids with the shit wheels? Your dad's face when me and Jimmy nicked them tyres off that Escort and swapped them over. He came after us screaming blue murder. I fucking legged it, mate. Remember? Me and Jimmy scrambled over that wall on Taunton Street and heard you laughing and shouting. 'Leave them, Dad! I asked them to!'

Them were the days, eh, Bobby? Look, hang on a minute.

Let me just . . . your mouth needs a wipe. There you go. That's better.

No worries, Bobby, mate. I heard you weren't well. Stovie told me. Said that brace is permanent now. Bit shit, Bob. Feel for you, mate. Anyway, looks like your carer's here.

Hello, nice to meet you. Yeah, me and Bobby go back years. Grew up on the same estate. That scar there on his hand, that was me trying to give him a tattoo. Supposed to be a rose but it just looked like a cat's arse, didn't it, Bob? Faded now, thank fuck.

Anyway, good to see you, Bobby. Look after yourself. No racing in that new chair. We need to get that pint sometime, Bob. I'll text you, yeah?

Byron Francis

Lincoln Prison, 4 September 1983

Byron Francis wears his own clothes again but after thirty-two months his shirt is too tight. He has muscles now, and the shoulders of a boxer. His jeans, too loose. He holds them up with one hand while his possessions are fed to him across the metal table. A watch. A plastic car. Four pounds seventy-two pence. He puts everything in a brown bag and rolls the top over.

He signs two pieces of paper and nods to the guard, who wishes him good luck. He stands at the gate with another man who whistles and sways from left to right, tapping an identical bag against his leg. Byron makes no noise because, since he's been in Lincoln Prison, he doesn't open his mouth if he doesn't have to. The air in prison is not the same as the air outside. It is tainted, like the food and drinking water, like the soap in the showers, and the rain that falls in the exercise yard. Byron Francis will never come back.

He knows, as a final flex of their muscles, the guards like to make prisoners wait on their last day, so he keeps still and looks straight ahead. Byron Francis can tread time like some men tread water. Most people don't know how to wait fifteen minutes, or seven hours, or thirty-two months. They don't know what the clock can do to a man. They don't know that there are cupboards and rooms, houses and gardens inside a man's head, if he knows the paths to take.

So, Byron waits and looks at the wooden gate, thicker than the mattress on his bunk, higher than a bus and set deep into an arch of yellow stone. It reminds him of the church he went to with his mother and, as Byron waits, he treads time backwards to the feel of rice paper in his Bible and the sound of 'Jesus Our Saviour' and the swell of his chest and the unkept promises to be good. He thinks of the back doors of shops, of broken windows and the shelves he stole from, liquor, cigarettes, stupid things, drunken things.

The whistling man behind Byron kicks a stone that ricochets off the high, curving wall of Lincoln Prison. Byron turns and looks at him. The whistling man falls silent, lights a cigarette. Byron knows that the man worries, that he wants the guards to hurry up, that calendar mistakes are often made, that hope is cruel. But he has no comfort to offer so turns back to the gate and the curving wall, to the towers and turrets, the diamond patterns in the red-brick castle.

As he waits for the key to turn, he treads time, backwards again to the feel of his new baby and the lightness of the soft brown skull no bigger than the palm of his hand and the swell of his chest and the silent plans he made.

It begins to drizzle. Byron Francis has no coat. It was summer when they put him away. He was lying on the sofa in his auntie's house when the front door flattened in the hallway and they swarmed in like black beetles, some with guns. His aunt crouched down like a beggar and pleaded. Byron Francis was not a dangerous man then.

Suddenly the gate is open and Byron is out. He is free. His trousers catch on the muddying gravel in the street outside and he hikes them high. He sees Trooper leaning on a car bonnet with a newspaper, sees he has grown fatter still, scruffier still. Trooper has the paper up close and mouths the words he reads. Byron opens the passenger door and Trooper looks up and smiles.

The car smells of cigarettes and Trooper's breath. Byron doesn't want to be reminded of his cell, so he winds the window down and taps the side panel of the car with the flat of his hand. The rain is cold on his skin. Trooper passes him a sandwich.

'Nice,' Byron says and settles the food on his lap. Trooper reaches to the back seat and snags three cans of lager by a plastic ring. He holds them up like a lantern.

'Yeah?' he asks.

'Nah,' says Byron. 'No more. I'm done with that.'

'Right,' says Trooper and starts the car.

It's twenty minutes to the motorway, then Trooper will drive fast. Three hours and forty-five minutes to Roman Road. There are girls and women everywhere, in blouses that pull across their breasts, and jeans that strain against their hips, squeeze between their legs.

A pregnant girl crosses the road in front of Trooper's car; Byron closes his eyes until he is sure she is gone. He won't think about seeing Carol or what she'll say and what words might come out of his mouth. He won't think of Leon. He won't think of the other child she has, the one that must be walking by now. Trooper is quiet, so Byron treads time.

The city thins out. Slack wires droop between grey pylons

in fresh green fields. Here and there, patches of luminous yellow sing against the white-blue sky and, almost out of sight, he sees a far-off tractor in a far-off field. Byron Francis has never ploughed or even walked a country road, but he knows the smell of wet grass and turned earth, so he treads time across the acres and becomes a farmer. At the end of the day, he climbs down from the tractor cab and walks across a swept yard, opens the door and calls. He sits at the scrubbed table and eats the dinner she puts before him, while his boy plays with the toys they made together, a train, a truck, a pull-along dog. His woman chides him for his dirty hands and wet boots on her clean floor, and he smells her perfume over the smell of his food, and wants her, like she wants him, then Trooper speaks.

'Listen, Byron, your auntie says to bring you straight home.'

'Stop at the shop. I want to get something for Leon.'

'She made me swear, Byron.'

The last time Byron Francis saw Carol, she was already getting big. He kept her lonely and he knows it. Never turned up when he said. But still, even when people were telling him she was running around with a white man, he thought she was just passing time. Nothing serious. He thought his son and his woman kept a space for him, that he lay between them, cradled them in his arms. He thought there were years left together, presents to unwrap and idle Sundays that would stretch on for ever.

Trooper pulls up and stops the car. Byron doesn't move.

'Listen, man,' says Trooper, 'I'm not going against orders. She told me to bring you straight here.'

They walk together to the front door and, when it opens, Byron steps in.

'Come later, Trooper,' says the woman as she shuts him out. 'Not now.'

Byron stands in the hallway and takes the towel she gives him. He hands her the paper bag and he walks upstairs.

'There's plenty of hot water,' she calls after him, 'and some clothes on your bed.'

There is quiet in the house, there is the warm cocoon of the bath and a drop in his shoulders.

He comes back to the kitchen.

'Sit,' she says and as she passes behind him she touches the top of his head. His locks have been shorn and his scalp shows through the stubble of new growth.

'Looks better,' she says.

She puts an oval plate in front of him and unpeels the loose foil lid. He hasn't smelt it until now, the coconut in the rice and the slick, orange, fragrant oil on the meat. She throws a tea towel on his lap and sits opposite him, her hands clasped, resting on the tablecloth.

She watches him eat with her head on one side.

'It's good,' he says.

'I know,' she answers.

She passes him bread for the juices and a glass of ginger beer at the end. He sits back so she can start, but she is different this time. Her anger is gone.

'I love you, Byron,' she says. 'And now my sister is dead, you belong to me.'

He says nothing.

'This country hasn't been good for us.'

He nods.

'You see the fighting on the streets? You see a police-man dead? You see what they're saying about black people, Byron? You see what they have done to we?'

She has the beginning of tears in her voice. She gets up and stands at the sink, turns her back on him, clears her throat.

'I sold this house, Byron. I'm going home. You're coming with me.'

Byron looks up, but he can't see her face.

'You remember Antigua?' she says.

'Yes,' he says.

'What you remember?'

He closes his eyes.

'The sun. The waterfall by Granny's house. Fishing.'

'What else?'

He remembers sleeping on a hard bed with the window open and a cool breeze on his damp skin. He remembers sitting between two uncles for a photograph and the white tiles on the church roof. He remembers cousins and ever-lasting skies and food that burst his belly. He remembers a cupboard full of sweets. He begins to smile.

'Granny smacked me.'

'You don't steal food, Byron. You ask for it.'

He shrugs, shakes his head.

'We're going home,' she says again and the smile leaves Byron's face.

'My home is here. I've got things to do, Auntie.'

She walks towards him and puts her hand on his shoulder.

'Listen good, Byron. Your place is all boarded up. There's nobody there. She took the boy and her new baby and she's gone.'

Byron feels the weight of the dinner heavy in his gut. It seems to rise in his throat and starts to strangle him.

'I couldn't find nothing out till it was too late. Nobody knew us, Byron, because you kept the boy a secret!'

Byron says nothing.

'Anyway, I had to knock on doors up and down the estate and ask people, but nobody could tell me nothing. One woman said she knew Leon, but she didn't know where he was. I went to the authorities and the council and everywhere, Byron. Nobody tell me nothing. Said it was none of my business. I had to humble myself, Byron. I did beg.'

She sits down suddenly, close, and holds his hands in hers.

'We're going home. I bought a piece of land by Granny. A nice piece of land. Wait till you see it, Byron. Flat land. Building land. And your uncle has a job for you. A good job. And you're not drinking any more. We're going home. This country has not been good for us, Byron. I lost your mother and I can't lose any more family. Never again.'

'And my family? My son?' he asks. 'You don't count him?'

'Listen. We go. We get settled. Make a good home. Find him. Send for him. Bring him up with his own people.'

Byron kisses his teeth, long and slow. He gets up, scrapes the chair on the kitchen floor and in ten strides Byron Francis is back on the street, crossing roads he doesn't see because he yearns for the feel of his foot on the front door of his house. If it's boarded up, he will kick it down. He will find Carol and make her weep for shame. And when that other baby cries, he will not hear it. And when he explains about treading time and the rooms and cupboards and the places in his mind he had to live in so he didn't go mad, so he didn't claw the paint from the walls of his cell, so he didn't tie the sheet around his neck and hang from the bars, all the things he has had to do to come back to her, he will make her weep again. And he will ask her for his son and he will kiss him and whirl him round and then . . .

Byron Francis comes to. He is in front of the boarded-up house. There is no one there to cry, no son to hold, no baby to ignore, no explanations to be made.

Byron lies between fresh sheets in his auntie's house. Night has come. He treads time backwards again and remembers his granny's kitchen. He nudges open the cupboard door and flicks the lid off the tin. He slips his small hand in and feels the chocolate, soft and sticky in the heat. He takes all he can hold, runs off, out of the swinging screen door, down the path, up now, curving around the fence, hops over the stream and sits in the shade, his feet dangling in the cold water that tickles between his toes.

He eats and eats, licks the chocolate from his fingers and squats at the bank to wash his hands. He lies down and watches the torn clouds stretch and disappear in the bright blue sky.

Mr Devlin

Dublin, 1952

Of course, every time it came, he felt it would never leave. It approached obliquely like a hunting bird and landed on his back, claws dug in. He called it 'the filth' because it was impossible to wash away.

He went to lectures and washed his clothes. He watched television, changed his socks and, when he ate, he counted the mouthfuls to make sure he didn't starve because the only appetite he had was for sleep. He would mark time on the calendar knowing from childhood that the longest it ever lasted was twenty days and by day seventeen he began staying up at night waiting for the gift.

Oh, and when it arrived. Then he knew it had been worth it. This time and every time. He was strong and clever. He was clean and bright and had again outrun it all. He was made of rainbow light and longed for company. He read and wrote, he sang, played cards and rugby and debated in the Student Union with words that sparkled on his tongue. He sunbathed on an everlasting green.

In those times it was easy to understand the tides of his life, that the filth and the gift were two sides of the same coin, shiny and dull, and that, after all, it was sweet and just. He would ride the waves and in time he'd get used to it. By the time he was an old man he would barely notice the difference.

It began to wane and he tried to make it last. But every time, it ran out like honey in a pot and he would scrape around for the dregs long after he'd forgotten the taste.

Judy Sutherland ('The Zebra')

Shipstone Close, 1990

Judy really did have the chance to get married. She must have been something like twenty-two, straight out of university and working her first job at the council. Family Liaison Support Worker. Steven Lewis, he was called, and he was training to be a surveyor.

Seven months into their courtship, he met her after work and said, 'I've got some brochures. How do you fancy Portugal?'

This was 1970. You didn't just go on holiday to Portugal in 1970. He was earning better money than Judy, but all the same. Portugal. When Judy's mother was told about the suggestion, she hovered between delight, disappointment and suspicion. There was, after all, no ring.

'I've never been asked to go to Portugal. Not by your father and not by anyone else,' she said, adding jealousy to the complicated emotions that she would later deal out like playing cards, gather up, shuffle and deal again.

Judy's mother watched for weeks as her daughter dithered and spun out the decision-making, kissing Steven goodnight with the chasteness of a six-year-old.

'Go!' said the mother, possibly too frequently as she realized Judy was loosening her grip, letting him slip out of her hands. The end was inevitable.

Then Judy turned twenty-seven (no spring chicken), someone else appeared, name began with a P. Or a K. Anyway, he was nice and clean and called for her in an Austin Allegro. He was possibly a bit older than he said, mid-to-late thirties at a guess. Judy went out with him for months and he always brought his sister along. The sister was all lipstick and laughter, and the P or K began to take a back seat in the relationship, became just the driver as far as you could tell. He got jealous of the two women and lost interest and that was that. Again.

More than once, Judy's mother wanted to take her daughter to one side and say, 'Play it clever, Judy. Give them a little taste to keep them interested but only up to a point. Keep something back. If you give them everything, you're storing up nothing but heartache and rejection. Not to mention the risk of an unexpected bundle in the by and by. Take my word for it.' But that would be walking too close to the edge.

These days Judy works all the hours God sends, a distraction tactic as old as Methuselah and familiar to anyone with half an eye. Or half a heart. Social Services give her all the shitty cases, the worst children with the worst parents in the worst bits of town. She's had spit in her hair, scratches on her face, a ripped coat. She's had complaints made (more than her fair share), she's had no thanks from the powers that be, just promotions on the promise of more money and less hours and it all comes to nothing.

She gives her life to those foster kids and if she'd stuck with Steven Lewis she'd have had a couple of well-born, lovely little ones of her own and not be worrying about the twelve-year-old girl that got pregnant for Uncle Martin or Delroy with the one eye who won't come out of his room. She'd have a back garden and lace nets. She'd have Pyrex and Tupperware and catalogues. She'd be softer.

Judy's mother unburdens herself once a month to the only person that would ever understand, Pearl. Judy's mother and Pearl worked together at the Transport Office, shared a desk and then lodgings, then a black coat when Judy's grandmother died in the May and Pearl's mother a month later in the June. They bought identical houses on the same estate and then the friendship seemed to cool.

No one knew why. Life just got in the way for twenty years and it wasn't until Pearl's husband had a stroke that they struck up again, coffees in The Devonshire or the Indoor Market on a Saturday morning.

Judy's mother links Pearl's arm as they saunter between the aisles, slowing but not stopping.

'Did I tell you our Judy's dyed her hair again? Yes. So blonde it's nearly white. With black bits at the side and underneath, here, at the back of the neck.'

Pearl squints. 'Why?'

'Same reason it was red. Same reason it was permed. She's lonely.'

The women end up, inevitably, in the frilly tearooms on the High Street. Judy's mother turns her inquisitive eye on Pearl who seems to be shuffling a lot, nervous even, turning the handle of her cup this way and that, taking the deep breath that precedes a good story but then just letting it out in a worried sigh.

'What it is, Pearl?' she asks, suspecting a new illness in Pearl's husband.

'Your Judy,' she whispers. 'Do you think she might be . . . ?'

'Be?'

'You know, "the other"?'

'What other?'

'Well, you know, she's never really made a go of it with a man, has she?'

'What do you mean?'

'And she was very keen on that sister. Didn't they keep in touch after the romance ended with the young chap? She used to stay over at your Judy's, didn't she?'

'I'm not with you, Pearl. Not with you at all.' But she had been with Pearl from the off. The idea that her only daughter and source of grandchildren might prefer women to men had been tucked out of sight in the recesses of her pride and social standing since Judy was a teenager and it was not about to be hung on the line for the neighbours to see.

Judy's mother took a savage fork to her custard slice, stuffed half of it sideways between her pink lips and chewed slowly, eyeing Pearl across the table with a hatred so intense she half expected the woman to burst into flames. She watched Pearl busying herself with the sugar bowl, rooting around in her shattered nerves for a route back to safety.

'What I meant to say is,' Pearl insisted as though the original suggestion had been misunderstood, 'do you think maybe your Judy prefers to be single?'

'Yes, Pearl. That's exactly what I think.'

They finished up and sauntered back through the market, both women drawing a veil over a conversation that had hammered a dozen nails into the coffin of their friendship, in concrete understanding that they would never see one another again.

*

Judy calls round to her mother's that Sunday. They eat their ham salad lunch on the veranda.

'Well, thank goodness for that,' Judy's mother says. 'About time your one and only day off coincided with a bit of sunshine. It is just the one day you get, isn't it? Can't understand that in Social Services. The office isn't open so why are you working, that's what I'd like to know?'

'On call.'

'What, every Saturday? There's no one else? Bit strange, isn't it?'

This was a well-worn path. If Judy had Saturdays off, then she would be available to her mother. But Judy's mother quite liked that old path and its smooth and familiar contours, and it was something to talk about at least.

'I mean, you run around all bloody day, Judy, and then half the bloody weekend, spending the last dribble of summer sorting things out at that Family Centre. I really don't know how many cases they give you and what sort of rota they've got you on but it's not right.'

Judy gets up, walks away from the table. 'Salad cream,' she says but Judy's mother knows it for what it is and ploughs on.

'You know what they'll be saying at work behind your back, don't you?' The last few words have to be shouted and then there's a poisonous pause while she has to wait for her daughter to return.

'They'll say one of two things,' she continues, her finger tapping out her temper on the plastic picnic table. 'Either Judy Sutherland has no friends and no social life, or she's too ambitious, or if she had a couple of kids of her own she might let her hair down a bit.'

'Three things.'

Judy puts her knife and fork at five o'clock on her plate. She sniffs, picks up her handbag and takes out a cigarette that looks like it isn't a cigarette at all. She lights it with a well-practised flick of a heavy metal lighter. Too shocked for speech, Judy's mother looks cautiously behind to make sure there is no one in next-door's garden.

Judy keeps the smoke in her lungs so long that when she speaks she sounds like she's being strangled.

'As far as numbers go, Mum, my caseload isn't much longer than anyone else's. Not longer, just deeper. I had two arsewipe fifteen-year-olds to find a home for yesterday, both with moustaches and tattoos, more worldly wise than you have ever been or ever will be. Then there was Crystal, 44DD biker momma liable to knife you on Monday, weep on your shoulder on Wednesday and offer you a weekend spliff for your trouble.'

Judy holds up her spliff like it's the Olympic torch. 'Thank you, Crystal. Except the other thing about Crystal is that all the time she's trying to be your best mate she's begging me to "Let our Kimberley come back home, will ya? Her brother can't sleep without her, if you catch my drift." Then there's the on-spec visit to the carers who by rights shouldn't be carers at all. The ones with the filthy houses that stink of beer, piss, fags and BO, where the kids sit stinking in front of the stinking telly instead of going to school, watching stinking adult videos with a bag of crisps and fizzy pop. And it's me that has to decide between the lesser of those two evils. Move them? Not likely. A move solves nothing, and anyway, they just go from one shit house to another shit house, and do you know what, Mum? Today is Sunday bloody Sunday and work can bugger off and all the kids can kiss my arse and the new crap admin girl can swivel on my finger along with the cheeky bitch that said all social workers were evil, and basically everyone, and that includes you, can fuck right off, right here, right now. All right?'

While Judy has been letting the smoke and the obscenities out between her teeth, and recovering her normal voice, Judy's mother has regained her composure and, with it, a decades-old memory of her teenage daughter sitting in her bedroom one Saturday evening. Judy's mother knocked the door and walked in. She didn't wait to be invited into any room in her own house.

Judy was crying.

'What's up with you?' said her mother. She suspected another breach in the fickle female friendships, the plague of every woman since Eve. 'Is it Kelly?'

Judy nodded and it was something about the admission, the curve of her neck, the bow of her head and the absolute certainty that Judy's life would be a difficult one, that made Judy's mother uncross her arms, gather her daughter up in a soggy bundle and lavish her with sixteen years of love and tenderness.

And here they were years later. Judy's mother walked to the drinks cabinet in the front room, took out two cut-glass tumblers and a bottle of whisky. This was not a Dubonnet afternoon.

They drank together. Each woman grateful for the silence of the other.

A few hours later, Judy went to the front door and began buttoning her new gaberdine mac. Judy's mother picked fluff from the navy wool/polyester mix, remarking

45

on its ability to bridge the seasons, turning her daughter left and right to check for stray hairs.

'Didn't that girl have a coat like this one?' she said.

'What girl?' Judy said.

'The one with the brother and the teeth?'

Judy looked at her car keys. 'Anne Clarke?'

'That's the one. You used to be friends. You liked her, Judy.'

Judy's mother folded her arms and waited. She saw Judy hovering on the cusp of confession.

Eventually, Judy sighed. 'I haven't seen her for years,' she said.

'Years? Time is nothing, my girl. Unless you're looking for an excuse.'

The last sentence was a question and no answer came. Judy's mother continued.

'You've got her number, haven't you? Bet you could find it, anyway. Ring her up. See how the land lies. Do it when you get home.'

She saw Judy swallow. And then quickly, unexpectedly, Judy threw her arms around her mother and kissed her on the cheek.

'Steady,' said Judy's mother.

'Thank you, Mum.'

She watched Judy's car pull away, hoping the 'cigarette' and whisky combination wouldn't show in her daughter's driving. The car's indicator blinked briefly at the corner of the avenue, then disappeared into the traffic on the main road.

Satisfied, Judy's mother locked the door and turned on the telly for the early-evening news.

Castro

The Ancestors

In the moment the officer's boot meets Castro's head, before he spits in Castro's hair and sprays hot piss on Castro's face, before that officer leaves the prison cell, we know and we are called.

Castro will not die alone. We will take him home.

He will not feel the concrete under his back, not the rupture of the artery that dribbles slow blood into the off-pivot of his brain. He will not smell the shit-splattered toilet in his dark cell corner nor the old smoke of sour tobacco that stains the walls like sepia paint.

We will lead him with unbloodied eyes through the terraced gardens of his childhood street where he runs with wooden swords and boyhood friends, a knight, a prince, a pirate. We untangle him from summer cotton sheets and rock him with a mother's hand.

We will take him to the foothills of a Caribbean island, to the edge of a sugar cane field where a free man works a ninety-hour week for a plantation king and dreams of better things for the free children to come. Castro, with a straight and unbruised back, sits on the porch with his ancient grandfather to watch the red sun smile on golden acres and he tells that man that he was nearly free and now he is going home.

We will carry him, unchained, past tall masts in a crowded harbour to the marketplace where another man stands in shackles, seven weeping stripes on his long, black back, and we whisper, we and Castro and all the mothers and grand-mothers, that we are going home, we are going home.

We will walk on unbroken legs back across the water. Not like that first time, that long time, when we lay in chains, skin to skin to skin to skin. Not like that.

Castro will not die alone.

He will lie, straight and whole, in the rich black soil of Mali, under an indigo sky, under a white moon, and when they come, the officer that pissed and the officer that kicked and the officer that sunk his elbow into Castro's throat, they will not find him there.

He will be with us.

Becky Finch

Staff canteen, Morrisons, 2016

It was the lunch break and I was stirring my soup in the staff canteen. The girls came in and they all started at the same time.

We'll get a sleeps-eight aparthotel in the town, they said. And then we can walk to all the restaurants in Torre del Mar. Linda knows all the best places.

And then shopping the next day and then a swim in the ever-so-blue Mediterranean because if you don't, you haven't lived, they said.

They said at night the temperature's in the twenties so you don't need to pack much and you can get away with carry-on, and for thirty euro they do this trip out on a boat to try and find the dolphins, but even if the dolphins are hiding, you get a hot dog with sangria, which is the best way to get over a bad head.

Then in the daytime, they said, you can just sleep and fry on the lilos because it's so hot you can't even walk on the grass and anyway it's too sharp and prickly, not like the back gardens in England and not like the wet, grey skies hanging like death itself over Milton Keynes.

Come on, they said. Come with us. There's always loads of blokes out on the piss or a stag night. You can meet them on the plane and swap numbers.

Linda will do your hair for you before you go, get rid of the grey.

We're not going for six weeks, they said, and if you go on the South Beach diet you could drop twenty pounds in that time, thirty if you don't eat fruit.

Holiday money? We'll have a kitty, they said. Linda looks after it because she doesn't drink, do you, Linda?

They said, we know you miss your mum, love, but it's not like it was a shock, was it? Didn't you say she'd been in and out of rehab since Noah put into port? You said you were half expecting it and you were right.

Then they all looked at me and I told them what Social Services said, that it was a miracle she'd lasted this long and it was only that I'd looked after her so well for so many years that she'd had a half-decent life.

I couldn't help getting choked up. And then it was like the floodgates and I told them what it had been like for me putting her first since I was six years old and never knowing what I was going to come back to, and I told them about the time she came at me with a knife but she thought it was a hairbrush, and that she kept falling out with the neighbours and they'd have a go at me and tell me they'd call the police on her and I'd have to move us again, and that before I got this job shrink-wrapping bacon joints at Morrisons with the best bunch of girls on the planet, I'd never had a proper home so I'd never kept any friends, and my sister married someone from abroad and doesn't keep in touch and wants to act like she's posh and forget about me. And all the girls rubbed my back and said, 'Bless.'

Then they started again. Bring a beach bag, they said,

and don't bother with sun cream because there's damaged bottles out the back and we asked Nigel-New-Manager-Retro-Flares what would happen if they disappeared and he said it was like a butterfly landing on a branch in Peru – if he doesn't see it, it hasn't really happened.

And we're drawing lots, they said, to see who asks Nigel for us all to have our holidays at the same time. Linda can't because she always goes red because she fancies him. Don't you, Linda?

Come with us, they said.

Nicola Wright

At home, Cambridge, 2011

She slips off pinching heels and a white carnation spray. She boxes her hat and thinks of a charity shop donation. Another woman will wear it next, another mother of the groom, the roleless one in the big performance. It was only hours ago she waved him off to new allegiances, to honeymoon memory-making and postcards home. Four nights in Lisbon, a week more in Spain, chosen and planned without her. As it should be.

Nothing left to do. Her son married, his cousins checked out of budget hotels, their tight shirts and new shoes packed, homeward bound, their weddings made and paid for years ago and evidence of their love slumped in booster seats, dribbling in the back of the company car.

'Bye, thanks for coming, yes, bye, bye.'

A widow on the top table, father and mother in one. Speech by the best man, another by the bride's father, and nothing from her.

She'd monitored, day by day, the transfer of her son's affections until the bride's triumphant final possession, no backwards glance or thank you to the one who loved him first.

Nothing left to do but remember. She finds it easily in moth-proof plastic packaging under garden tools and tins of paint, lays it on her lap. It's soft and blue and baby-shaped, as long as he was then, twenty inches? Twenty-two? It smells still of that other woman's house, of her soap powder and hairspray, of her baby shampoo.

There was a carrier bag of toys that came with him, a fluffy bear, a yellow truck, a plastic book with squeaky leaves, bitten at the corners. What happened to them? There were promises as well, to keep in touch, to never let him forget, but they were half-meant and not remembered. Only now she thinks of that other woman, big and ginger, teary-eyed, trying to smile. She sees her handkerchief wave, the social worker's comforting cuddle, their job well done and the child adopted.

She imagines the house that first night, baby gone, empty cot, just like the empty bed he's left upstairs. She thinks of the quiet and how that other woman must have endured it and she wonders why she never thanked her. She should have written letters, the ones she promised to write. She could have sent photographs and updates. 'Good practice,' the social worker called it. 'We encourage adoptive parents to keep in touch.' She wanted nothing more those first few weeks than to be alone with him, wanted the social worker gone, the visitors gone, her husband gone if the truth be told. She wanted that name 'Jake' erased from the documents. No. He would be Edward, he would be hers. He was.

She sits now by the venetian blinds. She will keep them closed for a while yet, like there's been a death in the family. She sips her tea and casts her net back in for another bite.

That last scene. There was the ginger woman, there was a social worker and there was another child, a boy, a brother. How successfully she's erased him. He was only half to Edward, they were nothing alike. That child must be married himself now. Children. Cousins to Edward's. He must never know.

She remembers mother and baby groups where she was welcomed and interrogated. Where's his real mum? How does it feel? Did you love him straight away? And the inevitable 'Aren't you good?'

But there was school and rugby trips and carol services and harvest festivals and sports days and two weeks in Mallorca and all the things that made up a life, made her a mother, no one could take them away. And one day at swimming lessons, someone even said how much he looked like his mother. 'Yes,' he said. 'I do.'

That sort of thing, mannerisms and accents and the way he held himself and his diction and his funny little habits, they can mimic a parent. So there was never any point in telling him.

Her mobile phone rings and she dashes to her handbag, upsets the tea, all fingers and thumbs.

'Edward?'

'Just wanted to say . . .'

'Can't hear you, Edward. What? Say what?' He's thought of her. She knew he would.

She presses the phone hard to her ear, sticks her finger in the other one, cranes her neck towards the window where the signal comes in, surely, nearer the airport, to help the message along.

'Yes?'

'Mum? Mum? I think I left something in the hotel, can you collect it for me? A jacket. Room 209.'

'209,' she shouts.

Then he's gone, all twenty-two inches of him. And the house quiet.

Edith Paisley-Jones (Woman in a Flowery Skirt)

Allotments, 1981

She hung on, love-ready, until her hands were weathered and rust-spotted. She stayed hopeful and optimistic until the light went out and the horizon disappeared. Her heels became square and sensible, her coat cut to keep out chills and disappointment. She wore thin lips and crept into loneliness like ivy through a tree.

Then he came along, and eyed her like an unclaimed prize.

She began to disregard her slip and umbrella. She found herself with him on piers, at funfairs, kissing him quick. She began to laugh again and leave windows open, became forgetful and blasé with recycling, a whistler, a lier-in, a gatherer of shells. Raising her head, she always found him there, waiting and dry-footed on the shore.

He took her hand, drew his shape on her life and on her plans. He was reliable and true. Then he became indispensable, necessary, and she wondered how she would live without him, and when he spoke of permanence and years to come, she began to suspect his sudden appearance and question her good fortune. When she had been eager and would have been grateful, he was elsewhere, loving someone else. So she told him he came too late.

Now, she was near-sighted and content, she weeded

her plot with rough hands, with knuckles too thick for rings. She became busy, practical, grew box hedging down the path and phallic gourds in pots.

She cut her own hair, silver, fly-away, untameable. At weekends she studied maps and drove hours to deserted coves and dangerous walks he wouldn't dare. She covered miles of beach in stout shoes and concentration.

He never followed. They never met by chance.

Margaret MacNaughton ('Pestilence')

Clarinbridge, Galway, 1953

In 1952, the drinking curse appeared from nowhere and took hold in Quilty John MacNaughton like cancer. For generations the family had shunned spirits, wine and beer, and instead, to toast special occasions, they took water with a tip of blackcurrant syrup for colour.

Even at fifteen years old, Quilty MacNaughton and Little Joe Kelly were hospitalized on a bottle of stolen John Jameson Twelve-Year-Old Single Malt and while Little Joe was discharged three days later having learnt his lesson, Quilty acquired, along with a taste for hard liquor, a less and less discerning palate, so that by twenty years old, potcheen had stripped the skin from his lips. His alcoholism could not be beaten from him by his father nor exorcised by the priest.

And Quilty was beautiful. He had thick hair the colour of new milk and eyes of the brightest blue, like someone held a lantern behind each one. Lying on his back on a bale of hay, as lean and strong as good timber, with his farm-boy tan, you'd be forgiven for thinking he was an angel resting on his wings, temporarily lost or taking a breather from the execution of God's work on a Sunday afternoon.

But his sisters knew better. Always and in every way

they gave Quilty a wide berth. Drunk or sober, there was an ugly meanness about him. He'd come home after a day in the fields, spitting and raging, cursing the stroke that had twisted his father's limbs, bemoaning the premature burden that made Quilty man of the house, farmhand and harvester all in one. He would wash at the pump and drip dirty water through the kitchen, spear the meat on his plate as though it had wronged him and gobble the potatoes down in three bites. As soon as he'd finished, as there was never a drink in the house, he would set off, hands in pockets, kicking an unfortunate stone the whole two miles to Hurran's Tavern, and afterwards crawl home to sleep it off in the barn. The girls had learnt long ago to bolt the door against him.

The MacNaughton household had resigned themselves to this life, the father to shuffling around the yard doing women's work, the two sisters to Quilty's bullying ingratitude, when again out of nowhere, Quilty fell in love with Hurran's daughter, Evelyn.

Almost overnight, where he had been sour and angry, Quilty became optimistic and easygoing, pretty-mouthed and calm. Evelyn hated the smell of the drink that saturated the stone walls of the pub and rose by osmosis up to the little flat above the bar. She despised the drunken fools that roared with laughter night after night beneath her bedroom, spending the rent, the housekeeping, the price of their children's shoes, while the till sang her a one-note lullaby. Quilty promised her sobriety and she promised him everlasting love.

After the wedding, Evelyn moved to the farm and

helped around the house. She made jam and meat pies, she fed the chickens, washed the linen and walked out in the late afternoon to meet her husband halfway. In his absence, she talked about him to his sisters.

'Do you know what he said to me, Margaret? He said he has his eye on the cottage by the south field, the one that overlooks the bay. With my money and what he'll save, he said that we'll have it one day, when the children come. We will.'

Or while she was making soda bread with Teresa, she'd use a bit of the dough and shape it into a heart, mark it with a 'Q' and say, 'That'll make him smile.'

The sisters in turn embroidered her tablecloths and aprons, they braided her auburn hair and took their father on day trips to the seaside or to Galway town each Saturday to give the lovers some privacy. On Sundays, strangest of all, Quilty and his father would sing old songs together in harmony, 'On Raglan Road', 'Four Green Fields', 'The Ferryman', with Evelyn balancing a little accordion on her lap and tapping her delicate shoe to keep time. The house and the hens grew fat under the extra love and care.

When Evelyn became pregnant, with Quilty working long hours to save for their cottage, the sisters sewed in earnest, bibs and shawls and smocks for mother and child. They gathered all the extra crockery in the house and began stockpiling preserves. They estimated window sizes and stitched heavy curtains against the damp sea air and listened in silence while the parents discussed baby names. Both grandfathers were christened Thomas, which was too old-fashioned, and there was nothing else good enough in either bloodline. This child would be special.

When Evelyn went into labour, Margaret sent Teresa running for Mrs Lewis. Quilty's father took his place by the range, trying as best he could to keep two pots and a kettle on the boil in readiness. Quilty was at the market in Clarinbridge. The special boy was born at three o'clock in the afternoon.

The house was quiet when Quilty opened the kitchen door. 'Hello?' he called. He saw Mrs Lewis first and looked from her to his family all standing in a huddle around the crib. Why had it been brought down into the kitchen? And where was his wife?

Mrs Lewis lifted something out of the crib and walked towards Quilty, who had packages in his arms and couldn't take whatever she was offering. He had a cut of coconut ice for Evelyn and, from a second-hand stall, a little plastic singing kitten, a toy, a joke. She would laugh when she saw it. It was hilarious.

Teresa was crying into the hem of her cardigan and Mrs Lewis was saying, 'Now, Quilty, boy. You have a son. God bless him.'

It was Margaret who took Quilty by the hand and led him up the stairs and into their bedroom. Evelyn's hair was wet and her face was white. Her hands were folded across her chest and bound with her rosary. The window was open and outside Quilty could hear birdsong and Teresa saying goodbye to the midwife.

'I'll come back tomorrow,' said Mrs Lewis. 'It's a terrible thing, that poor girl,' and then Quilty understood.

He sat carefully on the edge of the bed to not disturb

the blankets. And as he told Evelyn about his day at the market and how much money he had earned and what their total was, not enough for the cottage, not quite yet, Quilty was overcome by a thirst so terrible he thought he might also die, there and then, before he had finished all the things he wanted to say.

He looked at Margaret, who was standing at the door, weeping in absolute silence. 'I have to go out,' he said.

Margaret stood aside to let him pass. He held on to the banister all the way down to the hall and stumbled past his father, past sobbing Teresa, past the crib that held his special sleeping child, and two miles down the lane.

Five days later, Margaret opened the door of Hurran's and stepped inside. Conversation withered and everyone looked at Quilty MacNaughton and his father-in-law slumped together in a corner of the bar. Margaret spoke to two men standing at the counter.

'You and you. Pick up my brother and put him in the back of your truck.'

They were sober enough to recognize that they had not been asked a question and did as they were told. As the two men left, dragging Quilty between them, Margaret turned and addressed the tavern.

'The funeral will be on Tuesday week. Evelyn Hurran was one of us. The wake will be at the MacNaughton farm. Tell her father when he wakes.' She was almost through the door when she took a step back and added, 'It will be dry.' She was gone before she heard the collective gasp.

*

In the end, with no stomach to work the land, the farm had to be sold. Quilty insisted that they bought Evelyn's cottage in the south field that overlooked the bay and no one was to argue. The girls, their father and the child lived inside the house and Quilty made his bed at the back of the garage where he fixed the cars and trucks of local men, sometimes for cash, more often for drink. Teresa took a job in the hotel kitchen and Margaret organized family life, doing accounts for her neighbours, walking miles and miles along the shore with the special boy, collecting shells and driftwood, bringing him home to share his treasures with his grandfather and fall asleep on his lap in front of the fire. The child was kept from the worst of Quilty's rages, from the broken crockery and glass, from the drunken laments and bitterness that he aimed like an arrow at the boy's heart.

One day, when Bernard Holmes, the carpenter, knocked the door to collect his books, Margaret asked him inside.

'You'll have a cup of tea, Bernard,' she said, turning to the stove to hide her blush.

'I will and thank you, Margaret,' he said and sat with the child at the kitchen table. The boy was as neat as a button, his hair parted on the side, playing with a red tin bus.

'And how are you today, William? You'll be going to school soon, won't you? Are you looking forward to playing with the other boys?'

William nodded.

'And what do you want to be when you grow up?' said Bernard, picking up the toy. 'A bus driver? A fireman? All boys want to be a soldier these days, don't they, and wear a nice uniform? Is that for you, William?'

William shook his head.

'He likes making things, don't you, William?' said Margaret, putting cups on the table. 'He's good with his hands.'

'Ah, now,' said Bernard, 'I can help you there.'

That summer Margaret and William sat for hours in the carpenter's workshop watching him repair the leg of a table, the door of a dresser, the cross-beam of a plough, while motes of dust swirled and danced in the sunlight. William was given his own chisel and a lump of wood to practise on; Margaret served sandwiches and tea from a metal flask.

'I could get used to this,' said the carpenter, and when he put his hand over hers, Margaret knew she felt the same. She began to rethink her future. At twenty-seven she was nearly an old maid, nearly given up on, nearly invisible, but Bernard Holmes had seen her and he was a good man. She confessed her love to Teresa.

'I'm not sleeping for thinking about him, Teresa. I'm like a schoolgirl.'

Teresa hugged her and promised that she would make their wedding cake the best in the county, iced in pink and white, edged with velvet ribbon. Quilty was listening at the door. He stepped inside, stinking of beer, grease and sweat, and leant against the warm oven.

'He'll rue the day he married a MacNaughton,' he said. 'Nobody can stay the course.'

The sisters, long schooled in distraction, busied themselves with making the dinner and tidying up, but Quilty hadn't finished.

'Our mother was a whore who ran off to sleep her way around Dublin. Evelyn couldn't even wait for me to come back from the market to be out of it. Your man will do the same. He won't come true, mark my words.'

Margaret edged him out of the way. 'Get washed if you want to eat.'

Quilty watched her, his arms folded over his chest. 'Schoolgirl, is it?' he said. 'And wedding cakes? Ha!'

'You're in the way, Quilty,' said Margaret. 'William will need feeding.'

'Where is he?'

'Bernard will be bringing him home. I left him there for a little play.'

'Take care, sister,' said Quilty, so quiet and soft that both women stood still with fright. 'William is my son.'

Margaret put her hands in her apron pocket so he wouldn't see them shake. She faced him squarely and raised her chin.

'You've just remembered, have you, Quilty?'

In two strides he was across the floor and Margaret was in his grip. 'The boy stays here. He will have this life. Here in this house. He will have my life and his mother's life. Here with me.' He pushed her away. 'If you leave this house, you will never speak to him again.'

She turned to shout at him, saw his bottom lip contract, saw the narrowing lantern eyes and the promise in them.

She knocked his shoulder as she barged past, said

nothing to Teresa cowering by the door, nothing to her father limping around the front garden with his secateurs and nothing to her neighbours as she strode along the high road to the carpenter's house.

Bernard Holmes took her into the parlour when he saw her face. 'Is everything all right, Margaret?' William stood between them.

'I came early,' she said. 'And I came too often.'

'Not for me,' he answered and made a step towards her, but Margaret took William's hand and backed away.

'There are people at home who depend on me, Bernard. The boy and my sister. And my father too. People to keep safe.'

He stopped then and nodded. 'I see.'

At the front door she held out her hand. 'Thank you for your friendship and understanding.'

'They both remain,' he said and looked down at the boy. 'Now you, young man, you can still come by on Saturdays and after school. There's work here and a trade if you're willing.'

Margaret and William took the long walk home, around the wide sweep of the bay with the tide rolling in almost over their shoes.

'Why are you crying?' William asked.

'I was splashed by the waves.'

'Why are we walking so fast?'

'You're hungry, aren't you?'

'And why aren't you holding my hand?'

She folded down on to the sand and covered her face. 'I – I . . .' she began and said no more. After a few moments, she felt the boy's little hands stroking her hair, stroking her hair, stroking her hair.

'I'll look after you,' he said. 'I'll depend on you if you like.'

'Ah, William,' she said, getting up and brushing the sand from her knees. 'I know you will.'

She hugged him and they stood together looking out at the horizon that stretched to the edge of the world.

Trish

Hastings, Christmas 2018

Buy your usual size it said on the side of the packet.

Trish was sixty-two and looking good was taking more and more time these days. Twice the effort for half the results. Slimish she might be, but firm had become a thing of the past. Her body was letting her down like everything else.

A few months back, after she'd seen what it had done for a friend of hers, she'd invested in a very expensive elfin crop courtesy of Alex, who she'd known for years but who never managed to offer any kind of discount whatsoever despite them training together and working together for ten years back in the day. But Trish's chin wasn't strong enough and, really, for an elf, she had very frizzy hair. The crop led to straightening irons and straightening lotions and straightening spray and, all in all, Trish's bloody new haircut was just a very bloody expensive bloody mistake.

Buy your usual size it said, so she did.

The puce-coloured spandex Magic Knickers Trish slipped out of the cellophane looked like cycling shorts for a very big doll but there was no going back. She held them up to the light of her bedroom window. They grew no bigger on closer inspection. She pulled at the seams.

She held them flat against her stomach and saw there were two uncovered inches either side of the wonder garment.

Trish took a deep breath, positioned herself near the bed for safety and shook her head. If she died, she would be found in something she had vowed she would never wear. She would die of shame, but there again, she'd be dead already. Best to just get on with it.

She had to sit down to get both feet through the tiny openings. They were already snug and they were only ankle high. She worried as she writhed and wriggled that the Magic Knickers would stop the blood flow from groin to foot and she'd get deep vein thrombosis or gangrene in her toes. She wouldn't have to worry about being sexy then, not with one leg and no foot on it.

She managed to get the thing up as far as her knees before the hard work really began. Progress was slow. It was inch by inch, left then right, careful with her sharp nails not to pierce the knickers nor pinch her paper-thin skin as she tried to get a purchase on the silky elastic material. Still, she persevered.

She got them up to her groin and almost over her bottom before she allowed herself to fall gracelessly and heavily backwards on to the quilt. Her face was damp and her neck was slick with sweat.

'Dear God,' she puffed as she lay with her arms outstretched. 'I'm wearing a bloody tourniquet.'

Trish lay there panting. If anyone had been listening outside the bedroom door – not that that was bloody likely, but if they had – they would have assumed she had taken a lover, as they say in the books. Taken a lover. Fat chance. Trish tried to remember the last time she had made love. It wasn't with Keith. No. That was sex and it was all right but love it was not. Not for her at least. Okay, he was tender and knew what she needed but for pity's sake get on with it, Keith. No lie, if he had hit her, slapped her around the face once or twice during their sedate and silent couplings, she would have cheered. Bloody cheered. Sex with Keith was as perfunctory and necessary as a pedicure. You needed it but when it was over you couldn't really tell the difference.

Love. That was a different thing entirely. Love was what she had with Jimmy, sex or no sex. He didn't need to do a bloody thing, not a bloody thing. He didn't need to say anything, do anything. Just walk across the room to her. Touch her on the arm. Smile. Wink. Curl his hair behind his ear. Any bloody action at all. It was enough.

She felt a lump forming in her throat and she couldn't swallow lying down, so she sat up and felt the knickers cut into her intestine. She rolled them down a lot easier than she'd got them on and when they dangled around her left ankle she kicked them off into a corner of her bedroom where they crumpled into a miserable heap.

She walked to the mahogany dressing table and pulled out a pair of white cotton high-leg pants and put them on. She grabbed the black linen slacks she had tossed aside and dressed herself, finishing with a wide patent-leather belt around her slender waist.

Trish sat at her dressing table. Keith had been cut to shreds by the affair. He lost two stone in the same number of weeks and, even though she knew she shouldn't, Trish had been jealous of the weight loss. He looked handsome again, he lost his beer belly and jowls, but it was no good.

Underneath the neat-fitting jacket, he was still Keith. Jimmy buggered off after the news was out. Said his name was mud in the town. Like that was new.

But Keith moved out anyway, said he couldn't bear to look at her.

She can barely look at herself these days. No Jimmy, no Keith and the hair of a bloody elf.

Adam Albright

West Bay, August 2001

I did two things when I found out. I bought a pack of cigarettes and started walking. It was March 3rd.

My throat was raw and swollen and my feet the same. I remember a street corner where I saw a whirl of dirty leaves in the slipstream of a juggernaut and I thought about going under it. But I don't remember the rest of the journey because I had my eyes turned inside watching the two of them in our bed, my bed, and his hands on the skin of her thighs and the marks they made. I stayed at that corner for ever.

Five days later I knocked the door of my father's cottage and he moved aside to let me in. He fed me and listened and saw the lie of the land. He watched for razor blades and shoelaces. And though he hated tobacco, I never took a cigarette outside. I was an only child shared between my warring parents like an heirloom or a favourite serving dish, but he'd always been the sympathetic one, softer on my mistakes.

There were whole weeks when I sat in a sunken armchair too close to the fire, not speaking I thought, but he told me later that some nights he couldn't shut me up and had to leave the room to get a break.

His cottage was too far from the sea to have a view but

there were stubble fields for miles. The bedroom he gave me had thin cotton curtains that told the time. Mornings, when the sun rose, they glowed white and I would lean out of my single bed to tug them apart. If I stayed there long enough, lumpy clouds would appear in one corner of the sky as reliably as graveside mourners. There were days that winter when I lay and watched the sky turn from powder grey to bottle green and then to lilac, grey again and charcoal. Then slowly back again to white in the shimmering dawn.

But, bit by bit, my father made inroads into my grief. I remember digging holes for his new plants while he described the sandy soil with a science teacher's insistence. He lamented the things that wouldn't grow as we re-hung an iron gate, weeded the path, fixed the lock on the door.

I remember somebody's party where I shared my cigarettes with a new woman that I might have kissed or fondled, but I was drunk and never saw her again. I gained weight and words and circled again and again the moment I found out about her unfaithfulness, when she fucked him and where and how, and probably my talking was worse than the silence, so when the spring came, I found my own place in the village, four hundred steps from a cliff where, of course, I thought again about the ugly bounce of my body on the rocks below.

They would comb the beach and find me, open and empty like a house without furniture, and my father would have to explain what had happened and why. And she would mourn me then. I had other fantasies involving death and discovery, but the weather began to turn and

I found it harder to concentrate on them. I would watch the sky for coughs of rain but by the end of May the summer had arrived and the world turned blue.

I got a job that gave me a van and I would smoke and drive with the windows open, hurtling down high-hedged lanes and narrow tracks. I read my father's maps in the spare hours and found patterns like lacework between the villages and hamlets, shortcuts, roads that no one used. People waved as I passed and I waved back. I was quick with my deliveries and polite. I became known and liked, began to sleep at night. I woke early every morning to walk to the cliff for my first cigarette and, with my feet at the edge, I'd ride the nicotine rush with my eyes closed.

On August 19th, I had a visitor. She was sitting on the front step with a newspaper and I had a full minute to myself before she looked up. The light was on the crown of her head and in the dip between her breasts. It was easy to imagine what he saw in them. She stood up quickly and rearranged her features for the occasion.

I noticed her little suitcase and the current of helplessness she hid in her apology. She told me she'd taken up smoking like I had and under the same circumstances. She'd been replaced. She wept and draped a white veil over the past. She washed our coffee cups with the same fingers that clawed his back and selected memories of our happy times like an apothecary casting a cure.

It was eight o'clock before she heard the whisper of the sea. She followed me out to the cliff edge and offered me a ragged kiss. She slipped a hand in my trouser pocket and a tongue between my teeth and asked me plainly to come back. I drew away from her.

She stepped back and held out her arms. 'Save me,' she said.

I watched her for a moment, swaying and steadying herself against the wind, teasing to the last.

I turned and made my way home under a dried-blood sky.

Elisabeth Gräfin von Everstein-Ohsen (Mother of Andreas)

Wellingsbüttel, Hamburg, 2016

Forgive me if I stray from the point. Things tend to muddle as one ages and the exact sequence of events is harder to recall than might have been the case say twenty years ago. But of this I am quite certain: it was the clocks that told us, told us both to be precise, that Andreas was about to die. I had quite a collection of clocks you understand, too many to count, well kept, wound and maintained in excellent working order. So when they struck the hour, many of them chimed or tinkled or made music and in this way over the years I had a kind of continual symphony, a great comfort when you live a long time.

I had been sitting with him that evening and as it approached midnight so the clocks began and, quite without warning, Andreas opened his eyes and looked at me. It was the most pitiful thing, beyond upsetting, beyond agony, his and mine, because, you see, we had spent so long apart and there was so little time to catch up.

The first clock was given to me by my Uncle Fredo at a small party my parents had arranged for my thirteenth birthday. In Hamburg, in those days, a thirteenth birthday was quite an occasion; a boy becomes a man, a girl becomes a woman, whether she likes it or not. My Uncle Fredo was from Budapest and he ran an art gallery. The art gallery failed, as they all do, and so he took his pictures and opened a shop that sold antiques and curios. After a few years the shop too began to lose money, so he was bailed out by the family, my mother's family. Fredo was married to her sister.

Of course, I knew nothing of this at the time. I only knew that Uncle Fredo sat always a little apart from everyone and therefore always had time for the children who themselves were a little apart from the adults. So, at my party, when everyone had forgotten why they were there and had begun to gossip, the men about the prospect of war, the women about one another, I found myself sitting on the stairs with Uncle Fredo. He must have been only perhaps forty years old at the time but to me was a very old man indeed. He said very little, which was not unusual. He had a lisp. He simply put his hand in his pocket and took out a miniature grandfather clock no more than two inches high.

'It's from a doll's house,' I said.

'No, no. It'th not a toy. It workth,' he replied, so I held it to my ear and heard the ticking, faint and quick, like the heartbeat of a sparrow.

'Thank you very much, Uncle Fredo,' I said and I may have kissed him quickly on the cheek as I had been taught to do. His eyes were red and watery.

My uncle died soon after that or maybe it was a few years later. Time has an elastic quality when one is young so I may be wrong about the exact time, but I don't remember seeing him again, nor were we allowed to attend the funeral. My aunt, who everyone claimed had been a beauty in her time, quickly remarried. The funny thing is, that one of Fredo's pictures turned out to be quite valuable. All along he had been in possession of one of Franz Marc's earliest lithographs, *Sleeping Shepherdess*, and my aunt was able to reimburse the family for their many loans and restore her own, if not Fredo's, reputation.

Maurice was not yet twenty years old when we married but a man in every respect, having become the head of his household at sixteen when his father had been killed during the war. Maurice grew into the role quite naturally, taking charge of his fragile mother and overseeing the estate under the guidance of a guardian. As well as that, he had become quite a dandy. It was a fashion in those days to encourage curls if one had them naturally and to create them if not. I was fortunate in that respect and still am, as you see. Maurice swore his sister's maid to secrecy and paid her to pin his hair in tight coils every night and apply a mixture of sugar water and starch on the resultant waves in the morning.

We honeymooned in Avignon in March. It rained every day and the evenings were damp and dark. I woke before him one morning and saw his hair on the pillow, long and straight, and realized. I couldn't afford to think ill of him so soon and reasoned myself back into equanimity. I wore lipstick and powder and perfume, did I not? Wasn't I as vain? Of course, I was naive, but who is not at eighteen? Yet inevitably, it became one of the unspoken things between us, the curls that disappeared in France, the lipstick and powder I gave up when we returned home.

Since then, and until he died, we were never apart, not for a night, not for an evening. We slept for thirty-nine years in the same bed whether here or in Paris, or in

Vienna, in Port Elizabeth, Malmö, all sorts of places all over the world. Maurice liked to travel and so, freed from the burden of having to make our living as others do, both of us having been born to relatively wealthy families, we were able to pursue our interests, his painting and writing and my garden and my clocks, my silly little things as he called them, my trinkets. He liked to keep an eye on me.

My beautiful, beautiful Andreas was born within the year. I was, I am not ashamed to say, involved with him more than was expected or considered proper. Maurice complained bitterly and I was often forced to choose between kissing Andreas goodnight and sitting with Maurice in the drawing room, playing cards or reading to him, or sometimes playing the piano. Greta would bring Andreas in before bedtime and Maurice would speak to him a little, then we would share a few moments before he was taken away again.

His fits began before he was seven, just before he was leaving for school in Vienna. I wasn't there. Maurice and I were in the Tyrol staying with some friends. By the time we returned, Andreas was quite well and the doctor told us that in all probability he had become overexcited or had overheated and that we could be quite confident that it was a childhood ailment, a singular episode that would not return.

The school telephoned the house when it happened again and he was brought all the way home by car at an expense Maurice believed was excessive, but I was relieved. I was confident that with him at home I could keep him safe, seeing him every day for the few months when we were not out of the country. I began to take an interest in the grounds and the gardens and together with Andreas made plans to revive the spring meadow near the lake. There was a worker, a very gentle man who looked after the grounds in those days. He lived on the estate with wife and son, and he and I often talked about bulbs and wildflowers while the children played around us, or Andreas would run off to the gardener's cottage and run back again hours later, scratched and dirty. There were years, three or four, when Andreas was well, as sound and healthy as any normal boy.

Of course, neither Maurice nor I had ever witnessed an epileptic fit although naturally one had heard of such things and read about them in the newspapers. To be present is quite, quite different. Afterwards, when he was still and quiet, before the doctor came, I remember thinking that my life up until that point had all taken place in slow motion, behind a screen as it were, and that this illness, this event, witnessing one's child writhing and bucking like a wounded horse, had thrown everything into sharp relief. It was as though someone had suddenly turned the lights on and I had seen the truth about the world, and the truth was grotesque.

Then with the onset of puberty the fits began in earnest. They could be precipitated by anything, by hunger or thirst, by boredom or excitement, by a sharp word, a bout of laughter, by my sudden absence.

Once, when the house was full of visitors – I think it was Maurice's birthday – Andreas was allowed to spend the night with the gardener's boy, Karl. It took two days for us to coax him home.

By now my collection of clocks was well established.

I had always been Mama's companion on her shopping trips into Hamburg. She was well known to the jewellers on Jungfernsteig, who would display certain pieces that they had set aside for her visit. The owner and his assistant would cluster about her until I was completely forgotten and I could have the shop to myself, walking among the many cabinets displaying beautiful vases, necklaces, pocket watches and silver goblets. I had begun to make judicious purchases, acquiring specific pieces over many years, choosing carefully by taste not provenance, shopping in small antique shops, always bringing something back from our travels, coming home and sharing my finds with Andreas who was an enthusiastic and knowledgeable accomplice.

He in turn would take me on a tour of the grounds and show me the things he had changed or wanted to change, describe the things I had missed while I had been away, the fritillaries in April, the foxtail lilies in July, the wild orchids by the waterfall. He spoke always of Karl and the great friends they had become, and by now, at seventeen, how he wanted one day to travel and source new plants and discover like an adventurer flowers and exotics that no one had ever seen.

Maurice caught us one day, walking together and talking like this, and I think – no, I am convinced – it was then that the idea formed in his mind so that after the incident at the banquet he was able to act quickly and I could do nothing.

It was New Year's Eve, 1963. We had only been home a few days. Maurice had by now published *Letters from a Black Dawn* and *The Lycian Shore*, both of which had been well received, and he wanted to celebrate. We had invited

Marcus Kharkov and his new wife, Maurice's agent, Edward Otten, and some of the more enlightened critics, our friends, of course, and many people to whom we owed hospitality. Andreas had been seated away from me, quite at the other end of the table, and I watched him carefully. The room was very warm; there was a lot of noise, chatter and laughter and so forth, and drinking, *natürlich*. Andreas's eyes were bright.

It happened too quickly for me to get him out of the room, although I did try, and, of course, Maurice was terribly embarrassed. Many of the guests left, some of the women were crying and no one really understood that the best thing to do was to leave him alone, not to touch him, not to try and straighten him out and hold him down. 'He must be left alone,' I screamed. I pushed them away from him and screamed and screamed and screamed and, in truth, don't remember very much more other than somehow my dress became torn and I tried to take it off.

A few days later, when I came to, they were gone. Andreas and Karl, both of them. Maurice assured me that it had been Andreas's own idea, that he had been hatching his plan for months, for years, that he would travel and see the world, stay with friends, educate himself in the art galleries and museums of Paris and Florence, stand in the temples of India and the palaces of Morocco, sail and swim and ski and dine in all the great cities of the world. And this he did, and never came home, not once in fifty-three years.

Maurice died of pneumonia when he was sixty. He was nursed at home, *natürlich*, and I spent many hours in his sickroom where the nurse made up a bed so we could be together as always. In the throes of his illness, under the influence of his medication, Maurice began to babble, making vulgar accusations as people do when their mind is disturbed. 'At least the boy got away from you,' he said.

Andreas eventually made a sort of home for himself in England. He took a flat in Mayfair and a series of apartments on the South Coast, wandering endlessly, not unlike his father. By then, of course, he no longer needed me. Karl had become his friend and confidant and by keeping Andreas away from home secured for himself a permanent and comfortable position.

He had been staying with our friends in Burleigh House when he was taken ill. I had kept abreast of his affairs, such as they were, through the network of good families that exists all over Europe. I knew, for example, that he had had two serious love affairs, neither of which had been consummated despite his reputation. I knew that his fits persisted and that Karl had become so adept at recognizing the symptoms that there were no more than one or two public disgraces per year. Marie-Anne de Courcy took a photograph of him at the Chase Ball in Belgravia and sent me a copy. He was still a handsome man.

It wasn't difficult to arrange for Andreas to come home once I learnt of his weakened state. By then the cancer had attacked his brain and he simply no longer had the capacity to object. He was beyond speech and in many ways beyond reach but for that short time, each hour marked by the clocks, we were at least together again.

Karl

Rue Lepic, Paris, autumn 1990

The balconies of the third-floor bedrooms of the Hotel des Abbesses were very small. So any couple that thought they could watch the busy road below or the city in the distance were misled by the two tiny verdigris chairs folded against the crumbling cream walls. Maria, from her apartment opposite, watched time and again as new guests tried to find room for two in the tiny space. She wanted to call over, 'Only one at a time. You can't both sit down at the same time.' But she never did.

One morning, as she was dressing, Maria glanced over at the balcony. A woman stepped out and started with the chairs. She was tall, good-looking with grey hair, well cut. She made the best of herself, a scarf, a hint of make-up. Elegant, polished.

The woman had one chair open and was manoeuvring the other one, this way and that, into the corner, out of the corner, sideways on, back to back. Nothing worked. Maria shook her head and went to make her coffee.

When she returned to the window a few minutes later, Maria saw that the woman was sitting on the lone chair and through the voile curtains a hand appeared and in it a tiny coffee cup, a golden spoon. She took it without turning and, when she'd finished, she placed it on the empty chair and smiled.

The following day, the woman stepped out on to the balcony with her coffee. She drained the cup in one, put it on the chair and smiled.

The day after, it rained. The grey woman stood at the window and looked at the skies. She turned suddenly and laughed, spoke to someone behind her, and Maria saw a hand, the same hand, turn her by the shoulders, and the woman walked away into the room's half-light, out of sight.

The next evening, the early-autumn sunshine compelled Maria to open her windows wide and drag a stool across the hard floor towards the brightness outside. The balcony opposite was empty, the chairs folded.

She took off her cardigan and sipped her wine. She tied her hair back, stretched her toes and tried to relax. She could hear someone playing a saxophone, busking for their dinner. She watched students and tourists hurry past towards the bars and bistros, to a rendezvous, a party, an impatient lover.

In the morning, Maria dressed and left for work.

It was late when she returned and she was tired. Karl was in town and he had called her. They met in his hotel room. He sat opposite her, cross-legged in the armchair, and took a long cigar from a silver case. He ran it under his nose and lit it with great ceremony. He smoked slowly, tugging from time to time at the crisp, white double cuffs of his linen shirt. He was in Paris for the opera with a friend. He told her he was bored and hungry, having missed lunch and dinner for some reason or other, and that he'd been lucky enough to secure a reservation at Le Procope for nine that evening. He told her what he might eat and drink and who might be there, the artists, the actors, the politicians. He told her that the following evening, if she was free, they might eat somewhere more local, a little Lebanese restaurant he had heard was excellent. He would be gone by the end of the week. He then fucked her so savagely, she puked on the pillows.

She took a taxi home, showered and, with her hair still wet, stood at the open window.

There were two little cups on a single chair; one had fallen on to its side. The dregs had spilt and dripped off the saucer.

Then out on to the balcony stepped a man. He was short and wore nothing more than a pair of dark, creased, cotton trunks. His distended belly was covered with dark freckles and where the weight hadn't settled, his skin was wrinkled and hung in deep folds. Maria could see, even from where she stood, that he had dyed his thin hair badly. Around his neck was a large gold crucifix that clunked against the balcony railings as he leant down, righted the cup and wiped the chair with simian hands.

Then the woman appeared behind him and exactly then the sun shone from behind a cloud, throwing a warm blanket of golden light up the street. The woman threaded her arms through his, rested her head on his shoulder and closed her eyes.

Maria closed her eyes against the glare. Then got up and closed the shutters tight.

Dr Robert Wright

Golden Vale retirement home, 2018

Scotland is perfect. No need to go as far as South Africa like some do. I used to get away three or four times a year. I was divorced as a relatively young man and you could say I got a little bit obsessed.

Moved up there eventually, to the West Coast. It's the kind of sport you need patience for. Patience and common sense. Normally, I had a rotten aim, but I shot a beautiful muntjac once. It ran for a mile before it dropped. You let it go if you can. Let it live a while more.

It knows it's dead and it thinks it can outrun time. We all do.

So I let it go, let it live a while before I let the dogs off the lead. They tracked it through the trees and found it, black-eyed and twisted with a labouring heart and a long tongue.

I stood over it, the dogs panting at my side. I didn't watch long.

You mustn't think too hard about it at this point. One must act quickly. The dogs got the ribcage when I got home and the rest went in the freezer.

It was a long venison winter, breakfast, lunch and dinner under a muntjac's eye.

Gayle

Eastbourne District General Hospital, 2 February 1981

The hospital was eating her family alive. As soon as they told her they were keeping her father in, that there were a few more tests, that they had to be sure, she realized that the grey concrete monster had been waiting down there at the bottom of the hill for just this time. It would take him too.

She'd worked in the hospital shop once, just part-time, after Kitty was born and before Max. But every day, walking steeply downhill, leaning back against the gradient, she felt herself recoiling, as if from a nightmare. It was a silly feeling that couldn't be explained but, nevertheless, she left after a few months. Now, of course, it all made sense.

The view from her bedroom window was Staff Car Park, A & E, Haematology, Out Patients, Chest Clinic. Maternity was round the back and that at least was something to be grateful for. Most people didn't want to pay the car-park charges, which were extortionate, so if she popped out even for fifteen minutes, she often came home to find nowhere left for her Mini. Sometimes, especially on a Sunday when extended families came to visit, she would stand at the window and watch them pile out. The straightening of coats, adjusting of scarves, the tugging at hems, the shrugging and shuffling. 'I'll carry those' – flowers, cards and fruit were passed around. Everyone wanted the props. She understood that.

She got ready, took her time. There was no point in rushing. He wasn't going anywhere. A blue roll-neck jumper, a long denim skirt, black boots, a polka-dot scarf. Mascara. Lipstick left a mark and was best avoided. The afternoons were the worst for him, the long morning behind, the long evening ahead. So that's when she chose to go. Her brother usually went in the evenings when their father was drowsy and distracted by the other visitors. Philip kept it short and talked about rugby, on and on and on about rugby. Who could blame him?

She sat down finally at the kitchen table and took the Rotring 0.5 Fineliner out of her bag. It was superb, needle-tipped and finer than anything else she'd found. She could get about eight letters on her forefinger, ten on her thumb depending on the word.

'Mrs Crisis' she wrote on her thumb. On her index finger she wrote 'Tap'. 'B'day' on her middle finger and 'Hove' on her ring finger because 'Brighton' wouldn't fit. What could she write on her little finger? Nothing came to mind. She stared out of the window. Everything was at its worst in February. Her father once called it an evil month. She wondered if he'd had a premonition. She got up suddenly. Time to go.

'Hello, hello, hello,' right the way to the end of the ward. A couple of new faces. She'd managed to find another word in the lift on the way up. 'God' for the little finger. She saw him sitting up in bed, bent over his paper. His glasses were too wide now for his face; the fat and the life had been eaten. Tufts of wiry hair clung desperately here and there to a liver-spotted skull. She kissed it.

'Hello, Dad.'

She made herself meet his eyes. She knew that as long as she could see him, really see him, he was not alone. He smiled.

'It's bitter out there, Dad. Wasn't this bad last year, was it?'

She took off her coat and allowed herself a long shiver. She fluffed pillows and straightened the blanket, taking her time. She buttoned the top of his pyjamas and, when she'd finished, she stroked the side of his cheek. Just a touch. He took her hand and held it. Her breath came short. Time for a word. She quickly flicked her left hand over. Always start with the thumb. 'Mrs Crisis'.

'Oh, Dad, you'll never guess what?' She sat on the edge of the bed, near enough to keep hold of his hand, near enough to block out every other thought.

'Yesterday, I was looking out of the window about half eight, well, you know what it's like at that time, if it's not hospital traffic it's the school run, and this great big four-by-four came round the corner, obviously never driven down the Crescent before, and bang! Straight into Mrs Crisis! Well, not her, her car.'

The hook was in. He was laughing.

'She was out like a flash. Literally, I mean, literally pulling at her hair. She was wailing before she had the front door open. "You've crashed into my best car," she said. Best car.'

She could leave the tale there.

He was off, taking the story and fashioning it through and around their first encounter, their first day on the Crescent when they were moving in and a bulldog of a woman came running over as they struggled in with an armchair. The removal van, she said, hand on chest, would leave marks on the verge. They all went to a lot of trouble, she said, herself and her neighbours, to make Greenfield Crescent a nice road. They had standards and she hoped that a crisis could be averted.

Her father had stiffened. A crisis, he told her, wasn't tyre marks on a verge. He put an arm around his daughter.

'If that's a crisis, missus, you need to get out more.'

The woman ran back across the road and watched the van through red-rimmed eyes for the rest of the day.

'She'll never get over it, Dad. You know what she's like about that Rover. Honestly, I can't see how she'll ever survive this one.'

She winced as soon as the words were out. Somehow survival had slipped into the conversation and the icebergs surfaced like horrific punctuations and stopped them short. She slid off the bed and took the jug.

'And how long's this water been in here? Suppose you can't blame the nurses. Rushed off their feet.'

The tap and sink were unfortunately at his end of the ward and she was back in two minutes. Carefully, she rearranged the little display, the jug next to the glasses, the fruit in front, the paper, now folded, stuffed into the space at the back. All done. She looked at her index finger. 'Tap'.

'Oh, by the way, I meant to ask you, Dad. You know that tap in the bathroom? The hot tap in the basin? It's dripping again. How would I go about mending that? Would it just be a washer job or do I have to take it apart?'

He wouldn't hear of a plumber so she knew he would have to take her through it, bit by bit, a diagram maybe and a detailed walk through his toolbox. Perfect. She stopped listening now and just watched his lips, nodding and agreeing. Kitty was born with his eyes. Deep-set sapphires, firm and alive. Kitty had been just like him. Serious and definite, nothing ambiguous, nothing grey. Silly really to say that about a two-year-old. Who could say really how Kitty would have turned out? Children change but she knew that Kitty would have been just like her grandfather.

The two of them would have taken that tap apart together, Kitty the assistant. Passing him the right tool. She'd wait and watch and then replace it slowly, carefully, in the right place. They would have worked side by side in silence. From the kitchen, she would have shouted up, 'Drinks, you two?'

But they would be so deep in concentration in the little bathroom with the sun streaming in and the window open and maybe the sound of the birds, so welded to the task, that they wouldn't hear her. She'd be standing at the bottom of the stairs, hand on the banister, waiting for a reply. None would come. She would shake her head and smile. She would half hear their conversation, a quick economy of words. Grandad would get up too quickly and his knees would creak.

'Put some oil on these while you're at it, Kitty, love.'

Humming away downstairs, Gayle would make the tea

and the squash and put a little plate of biscuits together and bring it up on a tray. She would push the door open with her foot.

'Rations for the workers.'

'Thanks, Mum.'

'Lovely, just what I need, pet. All done in here. Kitty's done most of it.'

Kitty would blush and snuggle into him. The sun would catch her hair. The light in the room was fierce. It was blinding. She closed her eyes and suddenly he took her hand.

'I'm all right, Dad. It's just February.'

Somewhere way off, she knew he was talking to her, trying to help, but she couldn't afford to hear him. She let his words dissolve, slip away. Slowly, so he couldn't see, she turned her hand, looked and said, 'Dad, it's Philip's birthday on the twenty-second, you know. Any ideas?'

She stooped, picked up her bag and brought out her diary.

'I've been scribbling things down all week. What about an "experience" thingy, you know, like drive a Ferrari for the day? Might be expensive but we could go halves. What do you think, Dad?'

He would think it was rubbish, obviously. He would prefer something practical and worthwhile, useful, necessary.

'No, no,' he said. 'Unreliable things, experiences . . .'

Books, rugby boots, power tools, she lost track. It didn't matter. After Kitty's funeral she remembered her exhaustion, answering a thousand 'how-are-you's, a hundred 'anything-I-can-do's, and how was she coping and did she want to come to this place or do that. She was always responding, replying, reassuring or declining. Finding the answers was agony, but the questions? She never realized how hard it could be to find the questions in the first place. Five new questions every day, five new conversations for her dad.

She was in the chair now, up close, and they held hands. He was getting tired. The next half-hour was going to be difficult. He would be tearful soon.

'I think you're right, Dad. I'll go up to the Rugby Club on Sunday and see if I can speak to someone. I knew you'd have an idea. I haven't been able to think of anything on my own.'

The tip of an iceberg.

'Need your nails cutting, Dad?'

She inspected each finger in turn. His nails were dark and yellow, coarse at the ends, but beautifully deep and curved, elegant like her own. Her father held her hands all through the long night when Max died. Max, her Valentine's Day present, had perfect, tiny hands but he was dead before he could curl them around her finger. When they laid him still and quiet on her chest, she took one little hand and kissed it. He never opened his eyes so she couldn't keep him alive even a short while like she did with Kitty.

She looked at her ring finger. 'Hove'.

'Do you remember Palace Walk, Dad? In Brighton? You know, with the sour bacon? Where I trapped my finger in the door? Well, you'll never guess what? It's for sale. Guess how much?'

Here was a game that could go on for a long time. He would come in miles under. She would shake her head until he had to be told. The old B & B was going for a million and a half and he wouldn't get up that high for ages when you built in sidetracking down memory lane. But he was right first time. Said there'd been an article on it in the paper.

Shameful, he called it, to think that people were spending millions now on houses when others couldn't eat. He said he was worried because he had no appetite and he knew that if he was going to get better he had to eat. He needed vitamins, he said. He shouldn't be in hospital with bad food and nothing to do. He wanted to go home with her, he said.

'Am I dying, pet?'

She thought of Kitty and her frightened eyes. In the children's ward when they'd done everything they could and she was just lying there, when there was nothing else to do but wait, she had climbed on to the bed and turned her daughter's face to hers. She had looked deep into her eyes and said, 'I'm with you, Kitty. Look at Mummy. Stay with Mummy. Mummy is always with you. Stay with Mummy.' Kitty smiled her serious smile and stayed for two more hours. It felt like a long time then.

'Yes, Dad. I think so, this time. I think so.'

She stroked his hands back and forth, listening to the silent monstrosity of the truth.

But, Dad, I wanted to ask you something. After I leave you here dying, I'm going to visit the graves of my two dead children, and I was wondering, do you think there is a God, Dad? Do you think Kitty's in heaven,

Dad? When he was dying, Jesus told someone that they would be in paradise with him. She'll be a skeleton now probably, thin and brittle bones, dust maybe. What's in heaven, Dad? Where's paradise? I'm not sure about God. I'm not sure if he turned his back on me or whether he has a back to turn. I think about God a lot these days, Dad, usually when I walk down the hill and through those doors to see you. I wonder about God and prayer and having someone to help you through life and death. And I hate him. But I wish I knew that God was there for me to hate because I'm not sure about it all. What do you think, Dad?

This is what she wanted to say. Those were the questions she wanted to write on her fingers. As she looked into the frightened eyes, she hoped that he would make it into March.

His pale-blue eyes were wet pools of agony. His glasses had fallen on to his lap. She picked them up, folded them into the case and wiped his face with her hands. Putting an arm across his shoulder, she drew him towards her.

'Come on, Dad. I'm here.'

She turned to look at her little finger, but the word was gone, smeared across her father's face. She couldn't remember what she had written there, her last way out. So she held on to him and said nothing.

When he'd finished and the other patients and visitors had stopped glancing over and whispering, she saw that her time was up. She always stayed an hour and the hour was up.

'Tell you what, shall I get us something nice from the shop? What do you always say? Sometimes, pet . . .'

'. . . you have to have a bit of chocolate after a good cry,' he added.

She grabbed her bag, took the stairs, walked briskly to the shop and was back in less than five minutes. He looked better. She broke a big chunk off the top of the bar and put it into his hands.

Cornelia MacNaughton

Kilcolgan, Galway, 1979

Cornelia MacNaughton has four pairs of shoes. Three black leather pairs she keeps in a dull polish, neatly invisible under her bed. Every morning she sits on a little cane chair by her dressing table, puts her shoes on and laces them up. First the normal shoe and then the one with the built-up sole; one and three eighths of an inch. She is thankful for the shoemaker's magic giving her almost invisible extra height. She isn't lopsided and she doesn't sway. Her mother would like her to diversify and try stilettoes or boots.

'Splash out,' she says, 'treat yourself to a pair from Downey's and pop them into your man. See what he can do with a feminine heel.'

But the girl is attuned to her irregular step, to the *tap-tap* of her shoes on a polished wooden floor, the one tap rounder, deeper than the other. She does not want to imagine the pair of stilettos that the shoemaker might create. She doesn't want to think about crimson, patent leather and a pointed toe. She doesn't want to think of one half of her red, sleek and sexy and the other half not.

Her mother calls from downstairs. 'Come on! We'll be late.'

Cornelia MacNaughton doesn't move. Her mother

calls again and when Cornelia goes downstairs to the kitchen, she sees there is a sandwich on the table, cut from corner to corner as though they had visitors.

'You'll eat that before we make a move,' says her mother, tapping the side of the plate.

Cornelia sits down but pushes the sandwich away. 'I thought you said we were late.'

'I factored in your lunch,' the woman says and holds her head stiff.

The bread turns to grit in Cornelia's mouth, but she drinks her tea and drains the cup. The mother presses Cornelia's shoulder and takes the crockery off the gingham cloth. 'I won't leave your side,' she says.

They stand together in a narrow hall that smells of wax and cabbage. Cornelia turns slowly in her good coat so her mother can brush her down front and back.

'Black shows,' says her mother. She dips her fingers in the brass font of holy water and makes the sign of the cross over Cornelia's heart. 'Not that you need any kind of a blessing,' says the woman. 'You've nothing to be ashamed of.'

Cornelia goes back upstairs. 'Give me a minute,' she says.

In her room, she opens the wardrobe and makes a parting between her dresses and skirts and takes out a white shoebox with a little sketch printed on the side, a cartoon pair of shoes. But the drawing bears no relation to the shoes inside the box: it has no substance, no tiny pearlescent beads shaped into flowers, no white satin trim, no sparkling diamanté droplet sewn on the seam at the back. No signs of extravagance. No one would ever know how beautiful they are from the rough black outline.

She takes the lid off the box and touches her shoes

through the crackling gauze of white tissue. There are sprigs of lavender tucked in the crevices but their scent is stale and reminds her only of summer's end, the black autumn, the lonely winter and the lifetime that she stood at the front of St Augustine's watching him walk away, her unmatched feet in her brand-new wedding shoes.

Again, she remembers the shoemaker's wink as he put the box in her hands. 'I have put a leather sole on these, my dear,' he said. 'Good for dancing.' She holds the shoes to her chest and cries.

Since she must go and it's a long walk, Cornelia will try to think about nothing on the way. She has become good at it. She watches passers-by, men with shopping bags, women in scarves. She counts the unloved hanging baskets in the front gardens of narrow terraces. A black cat darts up an entry and she knows it for a bad omen. The black cat is a year too late.

She leans into the wind that whips up Gas Street, that chivvies chocolate wrappers in between the railings of basement workshops and over the steps of Georgian offices. She hurries across the cobbles in front of the number seventeen bus idling at the terminus.

Her mother is out of breath and tugs at Cornelia's coat. 'Slow down, for pity's sake,' she gasps. 'We'll take it slow from here. Dignified.' She threads her hand through the crook of Cornelia's arm and sniffs. 'I don't know,' she says. 'I really don't. Tommy Byrne skulks away to Dublin and has the raw cheek to come back to Clarinbridge, bold as you like.'

'For his grandfather's funeral, Mammy?' says Cornelia. 'He has no choice.'

As they walk up the shallow incline towards St Augustine's, they are caught by the old MacNaughton sisters. 'Cornelia, this is hard on you, my girl,' says one. 'Come in with us and we'll sit together at the back.'

Cornelia's mother clutches her daughter's arm tight. 'We'll sit where we always sit, thank you, Margaret.'

'Good for you,' she replies.

They walk into the church together. It is full, like it was then. And the congregation is the same. There are flowers, as there were then. But there are very few hats and very few babies and that's a difference. And she walks to the front like she did then but this time she has the arm of her mother and not her Uncle Padraig. Everyone looks up as she passes but she's in black, not white, so they look away, not smiling as they were then. And she's only going as far as the third row this time, not all the way to the altar.

The five Byrne brothers have the front row. To everyone else the five necks look the same, but Cornelia MacNaughton has kissed one. She has felt that skin on the palm of her hand and dragged her fingers down over the wide shoulders and into the valley of his back. She sees him drop his head slightly and Cornelia knows the pressure is killing him.

It begins. Father Neilson's grave voice is the same but this time he speaks of sorrow and loss. Nothing about God's glory and coming together as man and wife, nothing about joy. Then Tommy Byrne gets up from between his brothers and stands by the coffin. A creased paper shakes in his hand.

'My family want me to read this poem. It was one that

my grandfather chose himself,' he says. '"Miss Me and Let Me Go".'

Cornelia's mother slips a handkerchief from her pocket and holds it neatly in her hand. She never makes a noise or a mess when she cries and she blots the water on her face as though it is sweat on a summer's day.

His voice is beautiful, as it always was, and before he sits back down with his brothers, he raises his eyes to her. He has the same look as he did last summer, when they stood together in stained-glass light and Father Neilson asked if she would love and honour, worship and obey, and when she said, 'I will,' Tommy squeezed her hand. She made all the right responses, clear and true, and so did he until, at the end, he opened his mouth but failed to speak. He shook his head like he was trying to shake the words from his mouth but then whispered, 'I'm sorry.' He stepped down off the little dais and walked out of the church with his back straight and his arms hanging heavy at his side.

'"Abide with Me",' says Father Neilson. 'We will sing it now.'

Cornelia tries but there's a cruel break in her voice. All the Byrne men get up and take the coffin on their shoulders. The congregation sings them out and as he passes he looks at her again. The want of him floods her face. The mourners follow the procession, row by row, into a damp June afternoon and Cornelia's mother raises her eyes to the sky. 'Not a pinch of sun,' she says.

They stand together on the steps in a cluster of mourners and he is lost in the crowd.

'I'm not going to the grave,' says her mother. 'They've asked us to help in the kitchen. Will you come, Cornelia?'

'I will,' she says.

At the Community Centre, in a big room of yellow brick and blue fluorescent light, long trestle tables of foil trays and Pyrex dishes huddle against the walls. In the kitchen, in a swarm of women, Cornelia butters bread, cuts cake, washes cups and makes tea. She hears the guests arrive, dragging tables and chairs into family groups, shouting their orders at the bar. Someone lights a cigarette outside the kitchen window and she remembers the dark corner behind the church where they kissed one December night. He smoked the last inch of his roll-up and flicked it off into the scrubby grass.

'Are you sure?' she said. 'I mean, you know, because of my . . .'

'Don't be so bloody daft, will you? I don't care about your foot.'

'Leg,' she corrected.

'Leg, then,' he said and kissed her again. She used to love the taste of tobacco on his lips and the little puffs of smoke that escaped between them.

In the big room, the band begins to play 'The Rare Auld Times' and everyone cheers. Cornelia can hear the thrum of feet on the wooden floor as the mourners keep time. She imagines him at the bar with his brothers and cousins, a pint glass in his hand, looking towards the kitchen because, after all, he loved her once. She knows what he would say, that it was a terrible thing to let her down, that he would have left her sooner or later, in a month or a year. That he needs her forgiveness.

Her eyes blur as she remembers him walking away from her down the aisle and the look he cast behind him.

She put her hand out, she dropped the flowers, but she didn't take a step. She couldn't run after him down the aisle in her new shoes, untried and slippery. What if she fell?

She nicks the knife against her finger and a noise of agony escapes from her mouth. Tommy Byrne's mother is at her side.

'Are you all right, Cornelia?' She puts her arms around her and whispers, 'I'm ashamed of him and that's the truth. He'll be off again to Dublin tonight and you'll never have to see him again. Go on, have a drink now. You've done enough.'

Cornelia MacNaughton takes her handbag, opens the kitchen door and finds a seat in a quiet corner. The room is full. Drinks begin to appear on her table. A pint of stout from the Laceys, sweet sherry from the Monaghans, a double Jameson from Margaret MacNaughton, who points at the window. 'We are sitting over there, child,' says the woman. 'You are welcome to join us.' But Cornelia shakes her head.

When the music dies, through the thinning crowd Cornelia MacNaughton sees Tommy Byrne standing alone at the bar. He turns and looks at her a while and then he smiles. As he raises his glass, the fiddler starts.

She downs the Jameson in a single gulp and feels the rush, hot and heady like the first time she was naked with him and his hands were hard on her skin. A deep, biting jig starts up. Another fiddle joins in, higher and keener than the first, and then a whistle.

'Come on,' she whispers and throws the sweet sherry to the back of her throat. 'Just do it.'

A hundred heels are banging the beat, down on to the wooden floor, up through the soles of her feet and into the valves of her heart. She unlaces her black shoes and tucks them under her chair. She opens her handbag and takes out her wedding shoes. She slips them on and stands up. It's thirty-seven steps across the empty space to reach Tommy Byrne.

Bridie O'Connor

Kilmore Quay, Wexford, 1952

There's our baby to think of, just born, just loved. But the water so deep and beckoning. There's my husband and our vows still warm. But the water so forgiving, asking no questions.

Ah, but there's himself. One moment a stranger, no more than a voice in the hallway, and the next, hat in hand in my best room with her, his nearly-wife, my better-than-friend, kisses all round and the kick of a mule in my gut because there he is and if there's a God he's a cruel one.

Me with the power gone from my legs and the knowledge, as sure as a seven-day week, that he should be mine.

'Where have you been?' I want to ask but instead it's smiles all round and 'Nice to meet you, Robbie. Was the journey all right?'

She's all pride and blushes. 'How dare you?' forms in my mouth but instead I bring her hand to my eye and marvel at the ring.

'Ah, it's grand,' I whisper. 'Congratulations.'

'Tea, is it?' I dance away with a smile that congeals in the kitchen. I steady myself on a table corner, on a kettle handle.

And he none the wiser, with his big-eyed love and easy smile, with the wrong woman and the wrong dreams and the wrong future. Blind to me, so kind to me, I could have cried. Could have died. Could still.

Because there are decades to swallow yet and might I slip and talk in the night, get drunk, confess? And the years might, after all, stick in the throat, and might it not be better to wade in one Sunday after mass, asking forgiveness in advance?

With the water beckoning, asking no questions.

William MacNaughton

Clarinbridge, Galway, 1972

It takes a man seven years to learn the skills that go into making a kitchen table. But it looks like nothing, a person would say, a plain top with a leg at each corner. Thousands there are, millions of them up and down the country. Breakfasts are eaten on that table, dinners as well. Fists come down on them and make the teacups jump. Tears too. Babies with their toys are sat on top, out of the way of the fire or the mopped floor, and in other times dead men were laid out for dressing, spending their last night at the same place they ate their stew the night before and broke the heel off a loaf of bread, God rest their souls.

And in this table, you might have a drawer at one end. And in that drawer might be the cutlery and the detritus of a household, a button or a thimble or something hidden right at the back because some kitchen drawers are deep, twenty inches sometimes, and a lifetime of secrets can be lodged in there against a father's eyes.

William MacNaughton was seven years, from thirteen to twenty years old, under the carpenter Bernard Holmes and not because he found the learning hard or because the boy was instructed badly. It was because William loved Bernard Holmes and would never have left had he not been made to.

The Holmes cottage where William spent his working days sat apart from its neighbours in the village of Clarinbridge. It sloped inside and out but not chair nor bed nor table wobbled on the uneven flagstone floor. Bernard Holmes lived alone and wore a shirt and tie every day of his life and a jacket in winter. Over his good clothes he fastened an apron made from the skin of a white pig, soft as wool and, on the underside, clean as a sheet. The front was stained all over with oil and the same varnish that clung stubbornly to his hands and under his nails. Glue had stiffened the leather ties into rope.

Bernard Holmes was a small man and by the time William was nineteen he towered over the carpenter, though never in his mind.

Their working days together seemed to William neither too long nor too monotonous. He knew that Bernard Holmes took into account his difficult family circumstances and allowed the boy his long silences and black moods. He never asked what was the matter and never told him to cheer up. William loved him for it. The two of them would drag raw cut wood from the farmer's cart up the track to the back of Holmes's cottage, where the workshop sat straddling the skinny river and the field that sloped down to the sea. They sawed and sanded under a wide glass roof so that the wood was bathed constantly in natural light. Holmes had the eyes of a priest, searching always for imperfection, but unlike the priest when he found nothing, his heart sang.

'This dresser might hide in a dark parlour,' Holmes would say, 'but there again, William, it might stand at a window. We have to consider the latter.'

One year, the last before William left, Holmes announced they were to make an oak dining table. You have never seen a better piece of timber, a piece he had put by many years before when he thought he might marry and need a bed for his wife. But it wasn't to be and Holmes said that the time had come for the oak to be given a new purpose.

'She will love it,' he said under his breath and smothered his confession with a little cough.

The life story of a tree, its happiness and unhappiness, is written in its substance, and the piece of oak Holmes had chosen for the table was chosen for the message he needed to send. All other work was to be set aside, he said. And William would be in charge.

'That way,' said Holmes, 'it will come from you and not me so there can be no misunderstanding.'

William danced home that evening, only nineteen but a man now. And as confirmation, he was, at last, to be in charge of his master. The design of the table, his. The choice of leg and joint, his and his. It was he who would cut and glue the veneer and ease the marquetry into its place. It was he who would rub the oak table down and polish it. He alone would choose the varnish and, yes, William MacNaughton himself would be setting Holmes to work at little tasks.

That night William lay on his back, placed his hands under his head and, with his eyes open, dreamt of fame throughout his village and amongst all the craftsmen and artisans in the west of Ireland. He would make a table to be talked about, a table to secure his name and his career, a piece of fine furniture that would take him to England or America, that would make him rich. And more than that, this table would epitomize the difference between his father and himself. One a brute, the other not. He slept badly.

With each step to work the next morning, he felt the weight of that piece of oak and his master's expectation settle on his back like a yoke of stone. He believed somehow that as he'd slept the word had got around the village that the apprentice William MacNaughton, son of Quilty, the town drunk, was to be entrusted with Bernard Holmes's good lump of oak and what would he make of it? The idiot boy, the sulker, the quiet one with no mother and the angry father, what joke of a table could come from those hands?

William was sick with the worry of it and prematurely ashamed of the piece of furniture he had produced. Before he could reach Holmes's cottage, his feet had taken him clear off across the fields and as far as the next town, where he stayed a day and a night under the stars.

The dawn found William wide awake and no closer to peace. He thought of smashing his hands between two rocks on the beach so he could never work again. He could say it was an accident, that he had gotten drunk and a cart had run him over. No. Again, a better idea surely would be to bash his head against a tree and show everyone his wound, say it had affected his eyesight and it would be impossible for him to start the table in this condition. He would need months of recovery. And yet there was a doctor and an optician in the village and he might be discovered in his deception.

William clambered down into a ditch and thought of making a new home there like the old mad men that begged at the fairs, the tinkers and drinkers, their clothes ripe with sour mud, their faces invisible under inches of filth, their wild beards matted and grey. He could make an early start on his new career, become a deranged beggar before he was bent double with age, and live the rest of his life in this disguise. His mind was alive with possibilities, all of them agony.

It was not yet six in the morning and William was freezing. And he was starving. He had eaten his lunch the day before and drunk next to nothing. He pulled his jacket about himself and closed his eyes, hoping a way out would deliver itself before it was too late. After a short while, he slowly became aware that something stood between himself and the morning sun and that someone was Bernard Holmes.

'Morning, boy,' said the carpenter and put his hand out. William took it, heaving himself up out of the ditch and sitting down on the dry verge. Holmes had food and a flask.

'You lost the run of yourself, William.'

'Yes,' he said and took the tea that was still hot and the sandwich wrapped in a cloth he recognized.

'Home is behind you,' said Holmes. 'And you're to say sorry to your aunt.'

They took a more direct route to the workshop and one that Holmes in his sensitivity knew would avoid the village, just in case.

The sun shone down through the glass roof. William saw that Holmes had already sawn the oak into planks, now lying flat and dull on the wide bench, six of them.

'Talk me through it,' said Holmes, his arms folded across his chest.

William looked up and saw the milk-white clouds spun out like fairy cloth across the morning sky, and here and there snatches of blue where the day was trying to smile.

He squeezed his eyes closed and recited like a prayer the steps he would take to turn the oak into a table for his aunt. But before long the words began to fail him and the plans and the order of things and the careful joints and gluing were back to front and the precious table was ruined.

Of their own accord, his fists balled and writhed, smashing again and again against his forehead where the confusion lay, where he kept his fragile pride and shame.

'I can't do it,' he cried, turning away from Holmes and the stretches of oak.

Holmes took the boy's hands and lay them flat against the wood. 'Go back, William,' he said. 'Go back to where you were safe.'

'Where?' he replied.

'Where were you sure?' said Holmes. 'Was it when you made the dovetails?'

'No.'

'Was it the centre of the tripod leg on the lathe? Was it there?'

'No, it was before.'

'Go back then. Always go back to where you were safe. Retrace your steps until you find yourself on solid earth.'

It was his aunt's birthday. The table was brought into the small back kitchen and a tea was made with cakes and sandwiches and a great cut of ham. In the end, no varnish was used. William and Bernard had oiled and sanded and oiled again, true to the long waves of grain that stretched and curved and seemed everlasting, disappearing underneath the tabletop and emerging again, one endless stream. The oil had found the gold and the blonde in the oak and, here and there, whorls of amber like jewels in a woman's hair.

The table wore a cloth because the aunt fretted and wanted nothing to stain or mark its perfection. She stowed her knives and forks in the deep drawer and fussed about serving the food on seldom-used plates. Bernard Holmes sat across from William and talked the family through his recent role as apprentice, taking orders from the young man who would doubtless overtake him. And then he broke the news.

'I will be away now,' he said, looking at the owner of the table. 'I have a sister and a mother to take care of since my father has passed away, God bless him, and I have no need of working any more. They have enough for us all. I wanted to make this for you, Margaret, and I would have made us an entire household of things. I had a mind to make a credenza out of mahogany, but I never found the right timber. And then this oak came to me years ago and it reminded me of you, the colour, the close grain this boy has found, and the shape of it. All you. I have a yearning for peace of mind, Margaret, and an end to waiting, and there, I've said too much, too plainly, but I wanted you to have this table as a gift. We would have sat at it and been happy, but it wasn't to be, so William has made it in the end and it's yours now.'

The rush of words drove the blood to his face and the man to his feet. He took his jacket off the back of the chair and shook William's hand.

'You have no need of me, boy. I will sell my cottage and you will find another job. They will be glad of you.'

He placed in front of the aunt a small, dark wood box that William had seen him working on from time to time. It was small enough to hold a ring or a lock of hair and was closed with a brass latch. Then he was gone.

No one moved. No one ate. William sat at the table until it was dark, long after the tiny box had been dropped into the table's drawer, long after the table had been cleared and a vase of flowers placed on a mat in its centre. The understanding of the years of loneliness that passed between his aunt and Holmes settled slowly, piece by piece, look by look, visit by visit, until William could have cried for his ignorance and naivety and for the two people he loved most in the world. He had known nothing.

He climbed the stairs and knocked on his aunt's door. She was sitting up in bed with a book open-faced on the eiderdown, in every respect at ease and reading except for her unnatural silence.

'Why?' is all he said.

The woman closed the book and shook her head. 'Things, William. Just things.'

'It wasn't me, was it?' he said.

She looked up quickly. 'How could it be you? What would you have to do with anything?'

'I just thought . . . I thought I remembered something.'

'You'll need to be quick about another job, William. Bernard Holmes might be set up for life. We are not.'

She clicked the light off.

'You can start tomorrow,' she said, but her voice carried not a hint of certainty nor conviction and William knew the truth of it.

He sat down on the side of her bed in the dark. 'Can you not go to him now?'

She said nothing.

'I'm going to England to try my luck,' he said. 'I'll find a job there. You won't have me to consider any longer.'

He put his hand on hers and waited until her crying had finished.

'I loved you more,' she said. 'And you have been worth it.'

Big Tom Fallon

St Bridget's Hall, Skibbereen, Cork, 1983

Wedding Speech

I would like to say a few words now along with my thanks to everyone who has come here today for my wedding, for our wedding, for me and my wife.

Yes, yes, you can cheer, it's my first time of saying 'my wife' but not my last, I hope. And anyway, I've been cheering inside of myself since this morning. I'm a married man now and to Marie Kennedy, my friend from childhood and now, yes, my wife. It's her I want to speak about, the woman herself, but as you all know I can't read anything because of my eyes and so I'm speaking not from paper nor from anything I rehearsed, though my mother told me to try and memorize a few words. I'm talking from my heart and when you do that, you need nothing but your feelings to guide you. So I'll go on.

As most of you know, I went to England a young man of twenty-one and came home blind. They said I would only lose the one eye but, well, the doctors were wrong. I had a good job in Birmingham, in a factory, and I thought my life would be there, I planned for it to be so. It was a shock to find myself only two years older, back in Cork, sitting in my mammy's kitchen with her guiding a spoon of porridge into my mouth like I was a baby again, helpless and good for nothing. In those first days, I didn't want to live, and that's the truth. Even as I'm speaking, I can hear her now at this table and I know she's crying but I have these things to say. The truth is, she found it as hard as I did.

Now that I'm better, people tell me that they feared for my sanity, which is no more than I did myself. What is the point of life if you cannot look at the pale green of the fields in spring and the white mist on the water and, yes, even the black of midnight, which is different, I tell you, from the black behind my eyes. Very different indeed.

I thought to myself, 'Tom, lad, if all you have is this, then you have nothing. And you may as well be nothing because you can do nothing. You will never work again and you are no good to anyone and that's an end to it.'

Was I years of that mind? I think I was. I cannot remember very much as I was under the doctor as many of you know and that time has all become grey to me, colourless and foggy in my mind. The blackness – though it isn't exactly black but still there is no light – is a terrible thing and so were my memories of the beating that brought the blindness to me. Those memories were the last thing my eyes ever saw, a boot as I lay on the ground, a man's boot coming for my face. And those memories would visit me like demons, day and night, worry me, not give me a moment's peace. I was tormented by them. And throughout that time my mother was as patient as a saint and I was not kind to her and for that I would like to take this occasion to apologize for my temper and thank her for holding hers. There you are now, I've made her cry again.

Paulie Nolan, where are you? You'll have to shout so I know where you are. Paulie? Right, there you are. Paulie Nolan is another one I have to thank. I don't know why and I don't know how he could bear it but when I came out of the asylum, that good man and neighbour came to sit with me every week while my mother went to work.

'All right, Tommy, boy,' he used to say. 'I cannot get a minute's peace in my own house so you don't mind if I perch on this chair and read myself the *Evening Echo*, do you?'

I could hear the paper rustling and he'd talk to himself about the football and the hurling, call down fire on the head of Liam Cosgrave and Paddy Donegan and every other politician up in Dublin that knew nothing of the real world as far as he was concerned.

Talking to himself he was, week after week, a right windbag and blabbermouth. No wonder they didn't want him at home. Yes, you can all laugh now but it's what I thought. I didn't realize his kindness to me, as good as any father, better than some. Until after many months I began to wait for Paulie Nolan and his *Evening Echo*. He covered the news from back to front until his voice was hoarse and there was I, not even capable of making the man a cup of tea for his throat. He had to do that for himself.

It was Paulie Nolan, God bless him, who brought me back from the brink and all the life I have in me now is thanks to him. So, I would like that on record this day and I would like to raise a glass in his honour.

Thank you. But I have more to say so settle yourselves down now.

Because of Paulie, I decided to learn to read Braille so

that I could order my own newspaper, to not be dependent on anyone, and Braille brought me to Marie at the city library. I was walking with a stick by then and could make my way from Tanners Lane all the way into town if the roads were quiet enough. I don't mind telling you that I was frightened for most of the hours of most of the days back then.

To begin with, my mother would take my arm and lead me and then she would walk behind me, guiding me with her voice, and then I was able to do it on my own. I found a new world through my hands, I could feel and remember the colours of things I saw and felt for the first time: the feathery leaves of a hedge on one corner – green; the soft, crumbling walls of another – sandy red; metal, cold and hard – a lamp post in white enamel; rough splinters on a telegraph pole – grey brown and sticky. And smooth glass and sometimes people I would touch by accident that would shift suddenly out of the way or say, 'How are you, Tom?' and me barely able to tell them.

It was exhausting altogether. I would walk in through the double doors and into the silence of the library itself with me huffing and puffing as though I'd climbed a mountain, making all sorts of noise. But there was a voice. And the voice would ask me if I was all right and did I want a glass of water. This voice would take me to a chair and put the Braille books in my hand or on a little table and that voice was another Paulie talking all the time to put me at my ease.

Months it was before the voice told me who she was. 'I was at school with you. My brother is Stephen Kennedy,' she said. 'I'm his sister. The one with the hair.' She'll be blushing now, I imagine. I know she will have her hair tied up in some fashion because it's wild and black, wild as a gypsy, and gypsy is what I called her when she was seven years old. Stephen Kennedy boxed me for the insult and, like all good fighters, afterwards we became the best of friends and he's at my right-hand side today, all the way from New York City. I know you can see him.

One day, after a few months in the library, I was finding things very hard. I couldn't read the words because I was just beginning with the Braille and I lost my place. I could make no sense of the dots on the page, cells they are called, and to begin with it's a very difficult thing to follow along the lines. I was still on children's books in those days and I was embarrassed about it, ashamed I was. My fingers couldn't find the right place and when they did the stories were so basic as to be an insult to a grown man, even one as simple as me.

Anyway, one day somehow the books ended up on the floor. The noise they made. I had a picture in my head of all the people in the library turning to look at the blind man with the temper or was the blind man drunk or was the blind man mad, and all my imagining made me angry and my anger turned into fear and the fact of my blindness hit me all over again like it had just happened, and – well, even now it's difficult to explain how a man can think one minute that he is sane and be convinced the next that he has lost his mind.

Then there was the voice next to me, Marie's voice. And whatever it was she said, she made my blindness sit lighter on my shoulders. I waited with her until the end of the day and she walked with me all the way home.

My mother was worried when she heard what happened and asked if she could collect the books for me or if they could be sent to the house, but Marie said no. She said that I must come on my own every Wednesday to the library just before it closed.

'I'll let you have half an hour on your own,' she said, 'but you must make the effort to come yourself.'

So I did. Every Wednesday I made the effort until it was no effort at all. And then Marie told my mother I had to make the effort to get a job. 'They are hiring packers at Lacey's,' she said. And then Marie said I had to make the effort to go out once in a while and did I think I would be forever sitting in front of the television with my old mother and the cat? She'd take me to the tavern herself she said but I'd have to make the effort to wear something nice. Then I had to make the effort to get to the bar and order two drinks and pay for them with the right coins and Marie said she would carry them over herself. Very good of her, I thought.

All that sounds very hard, I know, but nothing was as difficult as the effort I had to make to ask Marie Kennedy to be my wife. Harder than Braille and walking home with my stick, harder than hearing the conversation stop when I first walked into the pub, harder than putting my lip to the glass and hoping that I didn't spill beer all down my shirt in front of the woman I love.

Marie, why you have been so kind to me and so good to me and why you have decided to love me and put up with me is a mystery. I cannot see you and tell you how beautiful you are, though I know that to be the truth. And somewhere there is a photographer who will give you a record of this day and you will show it to people and they will see what I see if they don't see it already. Marie, I'm a clumsy man and I'm bad-tempered sometimes, and packing tins at Lacey's will never make us rich. I will never be able to protect you as a man should be able to protect his wife and I will never see the faces of our children. But I have something a seeing man doesn't. I will have no distractions for my love. I will remember you always as a young woman with a beautiful voice and that will never change. Don't they say that love is blind, Marie? I'm the only one here that knows the truth of that. Now! Listen, they are cheering us. Because of you, there is not a happier nor luckier man today in the whole of Ireland. In the whole of the world.

Take my hand now and stand up with me in front of all of our friends and family. There now! I have made the effort to kiss you and everyone is cheering again.

I ask you all to raise your glasses for my Marie. And if there is nothing left in mine will someone fill it to the brim.

Acknowledgements

It's difficult to say goodbye to people you've loved even when they're only in a book so it was a joy and a luxury to be able to meet these characters again and tell you what happened to them or what will happen, to add another chapter to their story.

As ever, I've had help, support and advice from all the good people around me and I owe thanks to my agent, Jo Unwin, and her team, particularly Donna Greaves, who manages my life with the utmost efficiency and good cheer. Mary Mount at Viking has the keenest eye and ear for a good story and has steered me straight when straight was needed and guided me around corners when that was needed too. Also to Karen Whitlock, copy-editor extraordinaire who knows my books better than I do. To Venetia Butterfield, a special thank you for commissioning this book of stories and for seeing the potential in all these characters to live again.

Thanks also for the big love I have always from Leather Lane Writers and Oxford Narrative Group, who I see less and less and miss more and more.

Conrad, Dean, Kim, Tracey and Karen, this is one for all of us and for Marnie, Vincent, Kaodi, Ella, Reuben, Harper and Vaughan. We're lucky to have one another.

As always, all my love and everything I do is for you, Bethany and Luke, the lights in my life.